WITHDRAWN

WITH THIS RING

By the same author from Severn House

writing as Jean Saunders

GOLDEN DESTINY
THE KISSING TIME
PARTNERS IN LOVE
SCARLET REBEL
TO LOVE AND HONOUR
WITH THIS RING

writing as Rowena Summers

ANGEL OF THE EVENING
BLACKMADDIE
ELLIE'S ISLAND
HIGHLAND HERITAGE
KILLIGREW CLAY
THE SAVAGE MOON
THE SWEET RED EARTH

WITH THIS RING

Jean Saunders

This first world edition published in Great Britain 1993 by
SEVERN HOUSE PUBLISHERS LTD of
9–15 High Street, Sutton, Surrey SM1 1DF
First published in the U.S.A. 1993 by
SEVERN HOUSE PUBLISHERS INC of
475 Fifth Avenue, New York, NY 10017.

British Library Cataloguing in Publication Data
Saunders, Jean
  With This Ring
  I. Title
  823.914 [F]

  ISBN 0-7278-4472-5

Typeset by Hewer Text Composition Services, Edinburgh.
Printed and bound in Great Britain by
Redwood Books, Trowbridge, Wiltshire

Chapter 1

The entire afternoon was more of an ordeal than Tania had anticipated. For one thing, she wasn't used to making speeches, and the poignant thought that it really should have been James standing here in this impressive hall was one to be avoided. It was difficult enough to stop her knees from quaking, with all these young eyes watching her, and this was no time for becoming maudlin. Tears had no place here in her brother's old college, where six months after his death they did him such a great honour.

Tania's chin lifted a little higher, and she strove to keep her voice steady as her blue eyes misted just a little.

"In conclusion," she said, in her soft West Country accent, "I would like to say how grateful I am to the governors of the college for conceiving the idea of the James Paget Sports Hall in memory of my brother, and my thanks to Sir Peter Forbes-Wilson for inviting me to open it today."

The granite-faced Head of Studies smiled graciously at the slim young woman who turned towards him in some relief. How like her brother she was at that moment, he thought, with the same straight back and sense of purpose about the set of her shoulders. Yet how delightfully feminine too . . . Sir Peter cleared his throat and indicated the cord Tania was to pull. When she did so, the small silk curtains swished back, revealing the brass plaque with James's name emblazoned on it, and the legend that his sister, Tania Paget, had performed this ceremony on the final day of the summer term.

A roar of appreciation in the way peculiar to the college reached Tania's ears. She smiled briefly at the multitude of arms holding college caps aloft, before the eruption of a deafening applause. She would dearly have liked to slip away right now, but there was still the afternoon tea with Sir Peter and his colleagues to endure, served in the Head's study by impeccably mannered, chosen pupils.

Was James ever this stuffy? Tania marvelled. She couldn't imagine so, although she had never actually seen him in college. She had been sent away to a finishing school in Paris while her parents had continued their own absorbing life, studying wildlife in the African jungle, only to die within a few days of each other from a tropical fever.

She and James had grown somewhat closer after that, though each pursuing their own careers. Tania clinging to the more sedate life of a company linguist, while James had become a renowned mountaineer, with eventual tragic consequences . . .

"This is a splendid, if emotional day for us, Miss Paget," Sir Peter, who didn't look as if he had an emotional nerve in his body, said pompously a little later, as the tea and thin cucumber sandwiches were ceremoniously handed round.

"We remember your brother with great affection, and it will be a comfort to you to know that his memory lives on in our sports hall."

"Yes, indeed, Sir Peter," Tania murmured.

Despite the solemnity of the occasion, she felt an

almost irrepressible urge to laugh. How many times had James mimicked this man's stentorian voice, and the hands-linked-across-the-abdomen walk! How often he had made her laugh . . . and how much she missed him, she realised, with a rush of nostalgia.

"I hope his companion has been similarly honoured," one of the professors commented. "I trust the French will realise the importance of the climb the two men undertook in such hazardous conditions— "

"Some called them foolhardy conditions." Tania had spoken the words aloud before she had time to think.

She could never quite rid herself of the bitterness she felt at the waste of a young life on a mountainside. Particularly when that life had been her brother's, and his companion still lived to tell the tale, and had cashed in on it handsomely, though so far, Tania had been quite unable to read any of the French newspaper cuttings that Claude Girard had sent her.

The photos in the cuttings, of the two tousled, smiling faces, with the snow-capped mountains behind them, had been enough to make Tania fling the newsprint away, her heart pounding. She knew it was completely illogical to feel such resentment towards Claude Girard because he was alive while her brother was dead, but it was a feeling that had seeped into her from the moment she had heard of the accident.

She suddenly realised that the studious college gentlemen were looking slightly embarrassed at her comment, and she forced a smile to her lips.

"I know how pleased James would have been about today's ceremony," she made an effort at warmth. "On his behalf, I thank you all most sincerely. But if you won't think me terribly rude, I think it's time I was leaving."

3

She was thankful they didn't press her to stay any longer. In this all-male college she felt out of place, and some of the side-long glances from the older students on her arrival had sent the hot colour to Tania's cheeks.

As she was escorted to her car by Sir Peter himself, Tania swore she could hear a subdued whistle from the ancient, creeper-covered building, but if he heard it, Sir Peter made no comment as he bade her goodbye. Tania suspected he gave as big a sigh as her own as she eased her small white car away from the grandiose surroundings, and headed back along the motorway to her small town flat.

For a nasty moment, Tania had thought the professors were going to ask for more information about James's companion, the dashing Claude Girard, and those were questions she had no wish to answer. She had never met him, and had no wish to do so. She had made that plain in their brief correspondence after her brother's death.

"I am so desolate that I am unable to attend the funeral in England," Claude had written in perfect English, when the news had been broken to her. "The doctors refuse to let me leave the hospital until the multiple breaks in my leg have mended, but my heart goes out to you, Miss Paget – Tania. We have both lost someone dear to us."

He had signed it flamboyantly, "Claude Girard".

The last sentence established a link between them that Tania resented deeply. She hated him. She had replied with a cold and distant letter in immaculate French, leaving him in no doubt that there was no further need for communication between them. She had loathed James's fascination with mountains. Now that he was dead, all her hatred was transferred to the companion who had shared his love of danger and adventure. It was one way of expending her grief, by turning it into hate.

There had been one appalling moment when Sir Peter Forbes-Wilson had approached her about today's ceremony. Tania had been furious to learn he had also asked Claude Girard to be present, and had replied flatly that unless this was a solo engagement, she would simply not be available. Let him think it was an ego trip or whatever he liked. Whatever his excuses to Claude Girard, the Frenchman would not be there, Sir Peter had told her, and Tania had breathed more easily.

Was there some small flicker of jealousy that this Frenchman had known her brother better than she did? That because of the lifestyle of their parents, Tania and James had led practically separate lives in their formative years, and only now did she really feel the pangs of sadness that they had never really been close? Only in the latter years, when it was too late to make up for all the time they had spent apart in their different schools, did Tania turn to him as her only living relative, only to have him cruelly snatched away from her by the mountain.

Yes, she thought illogically, as she sped back towards London. The mountain, and Claude Girard. But for them, James and herself might have created some kind of home life that their parents had never provided, loving though they were. She never admitted that James would never have succombed to such a cosy, domestic set-up either. He was a true son of their parents, and it was Tania who was the cuckoo in the nest – only in her case she wanted stability in her life, while everyone else wanted excitement. She shivered. Look where it had got them! Her parents dying in some remote part of the world, and James on a French mountainside. Her way was best, Tania thought fervently. Safe, and best.

It was early evening when she got back to her flat. The

5

city was hot and sultry, and for a few moments Tania thought how wonderful it would be in the country right now. She and James had been born there, in a little village in the heart of Devon. It would be good to get away. She toyed with the idea, not sure if she was merely looking over her shoulder, trying to glean a little comfort out of the past. She was restless, understandably so. Today, at James's old college, so many old memories had been evoked.

Her head throbbed a little. Before she did anything else, she would have a long leisurely bath, Tania decided. David Lee, with whom she had a platonic relationship, might call round later, but she hoped not. She didn't feel like company. It was good now and then, to shut her door and be enclosed within her own four walls. Guiltily, Tania knew that such sentiments were yet another throwback, rebelling against the outwardness of all her family. Sometimes she wondered if she was in danger of becoming a recluse. She had even voiced her fears to David one night.

"You a recluse, darling?" David's good-looking face had creased into a laugh. "I'd hardly say so, with all the VIPs you interpret for, here and overseas! What a waste it would be if you were!"

She knew he'd like to change their platonic status, and only wanted her to say the word. His eyes admired her, drinking in the softness of her shoulder-length chestnut hair and the unusual amber eyes, the peachy complexion and the full, mobile mouth. His eyes had strayed further, to the slender shape of her with its feminine curves, and Tania had laughed a little self-consciously. Workwise, she was hardly ever alone, which was why she valued her privacy so much, and to his credit, David never pushed her too far.

6

Now, watching the soap bubbles burst and disappear against her long limbs, Tania felt a renewed sadness for all the years she and her brother had spent apart. Nothing could change it now, but her memories of the small boy with whom she had run laughing and barefoot through the Devon meadows were suddenly strong in her head. She rose from her bath, pampering herself with her favourite talc, and swathed herself in towels, before pulling a cool Chinese dressing-robe around her. One of her parents' more useful gifts from foreign parts, she thought ruefully, eyeing the carved elephant tusks above the mantelpiece, and the Indian footstool that was too uncomfortable to use.

Tania was making some coffee in her tiny kitchen and thinking about preparing a salad, when the doorbell rang. David didn't take the hint after all then. She shrugged. Maybe company wasn't such a terrible idea though, and there were enough salad ingredients in the refrigerator to stretch for two. She opened the door of her flat, and immediately two high spots of colour stained her cheeks at the sight of the stranger standing there.

He wasn't really a stranger, of course. She had seen his face too many times for her to ever think of him as such. His healthy, rugged looks had smiled out at her from a dozen newspapers at various times. She had seen him standing beside James in snapshots, cool, self-composed, arrogantly confident. Claude Girard. She hadn't known how tall he would be, nor thought he would be as broad-shouldered. Usually he was smothered in mountaineering gear in the photos, but this being summer, he wore a thin roll-neck shirt and a light sports jacket over dark slacks. He looked very French. His dark hair curled into his neck. His dark eyes looked down at her unsmilingly, and they moved more slowly downwards, to where the shock of his arrival had tensed her body against the Chinese silk. For a moment, Tania felt like throwing her hands across her breasts, and was angry at him for making her feel that way.

"I apologise for arriving so unexpectedly on your doorstep, Miss Paget." The English in his letter had been perfect, but he spoke it with a richly attractive accent. "Or may I call you Tania? I do hope so, since I always think of you that way. It was impossible not to, whenever James spoke of you."

It was hitting below the belt, she thought angrily, dredging up James's memory between them as a way of introduction.

"Why are you here?" There was no point in being pseudo-polite. He knew she wanted nothing to do with him. Her own letter, and then the rebuff she'd given him over the college ceremony, had made sure of that. "I thought I'd made it plain that we have nothing to discuss— "

"You did. Very plain, Tania. What I want to know, is why?"

She stared at him. "Don't tell me you came all the way from France to ask me that!" she said incredulously.

"Not entirely," Claude said calmly. "But I don't intend to leave here until you give me an explanation why you continue to be so uncivil to me. I was James's closest friend. I'd like to be yours too."

The momentary silence was so charged with electricity that Tania almost flinched. This was the man she hated most in all the world. This man, standing on her doorstep and looking her over in a way she could only describe as – as sensual. Assessing her as if he had X-ray eyes

8

and could see right through the luxurious silk robe to where her flesh suddenly tingled. Not one of David's looks had ever made her feel like this. Never had David given her this heart-pounding sensation of suddenly being vulnerable . . .

Tania didn't like the feeling. She had always been very much in control of her destiny, despite the fact that it would never attain the dizzy excitement of her brother's or her parents' lives. She knew exactly what she wanted out of life, and it wasn't being made to feel gauche and unsure of herself by a stranger.

The young couple from the flat above passed her door, glancing her way. Seconds later, she heard them mutter something and laugh. Her face flamed.

"You'd better come in." She knew she was being ungracious and didn't care. She hadn't asked him to come here. For James's sake, though, she couldn't be totally rude to Claude Girard. For James's sake only, she vowed. She stood aside to let him enter the flat, knotting her silk robe a little tighter around her waist, and hoping he wouldn't notice. She was aware of his slight limp, and remembered the multiple injuries to his leg when he'd tried desperately to save James from hurtling to his death on the mountain. He had suffered physically too, Tania conceded, but her brief sympathy was quickly smothered. She had resented him for too long to forget it in a single moment. She guessed, too, that Claude Girard wasn't the kind of man to want sympathy from anyone. James had once told her that after a previous fall, Claude couldn't wait to get back to the mountainside again. Her brother's voice had been filled with a pride that Tania didn't begin to try and understand.

"Won't you sit down?" She could hardly expect him to

remain standing, but her voice was distant. She felt better when he was seated. He had seemed to dominate the small living-room. Uneasily, the fleeting thought swept through Tania's head that he still dominated it. He was that kind of man. His long legs seemed to extend halfway across the room. She took a grip on herself, forcing herself to be charitable if not welcoming.

"I was about to make some coffee. Would you like some?"

"Thank you, yes." Claude's faint smile told her he knew exactly how much she wished him out of here. She walked stiffly to the kitchen, plugged in the kettle and put two mugs on a tray. Her stomach suddenly gnawed. One cucumber sandwich and a cup of tea at the college hadn't been enough to see her through the day, and she'd been far too nervous to eat any lunch.

She glanced back to where Claude Girard sat on one of her armchairs. She had never expected to see him here, nor wanted him. At that moment, she seemed to hear James's protesting voice when they had run wild in the sweet Devon meadows, telling her not to be so grouchy. Tania bit her lip, remembering that this was James's friend, and poked her head into the living-room.

"Have you eaten – Claude?" she said abruptly. "I was about to have a salad and cold meat. If you'd like some— "

"Yes please. Anything would be fine. I was going to ask you out for a meal— "

"It's all right. The salad's ready." She didn't want to be obligated to him by going to a restaurant with him. And she couldn't wait that long anyway. She was too ravenous. She should get some clothes on . . . but that would take time too, and Tania was beginning to feel decidedly light-headed. Maybe it was only partly lack of food. That, and the emotional day, and now the appearance of Claude Girard, was turning her world upside down. The sooner they ate and she got rid of him, the better.

Avoiding the thought that they looked a very cosy two-some, eating a meal together and with Tania wearing only the Chinese robe, she thought grimly that the situation was anything but comfortable. She realised that Claude was a little embarrassed at being here too, despite his masculine air of self-confidence. Serves him right, she thought. She hadn't asked him to come.

"You must have known that we had to talk," Claude said suddenly. They had eaten the salad, and she had brought cheese and biscuits to the table and topped up their coffee mugs.

"I don't see why. James and I never interfered in each others' lives. He thought what I do is tame, and I could never sanction the kind of life he led."

"You make it sound immoral." Claude was suddenly amused, and Tania realised that in criticising James, she criticised Claude too. She didn't let it worry her.

"Not immoral. Just heedless of other people's feelings and wishes," she said pointedly.

'Meaning yours, I suppose. Do you think you had any right to question what he did with his life, any more than he questioned what you did with yours?"

Tania glared at him. "I would have expected you to speak the way James did," she said scathingly. "It's a very selfish attitude to think that one person's life is totally complete in itself. It isn't. It touches other people, brings them hurt and disillusionment."

"I know about your background, Tania." Claude's voice

was suddenly gentle, caring even. "James and I had many lonely hours to discuss how we would change the world if we could. It must have been a strange sort of childhood after the early years, with your parents pursuing their own interests so much."

Far from warming to him at this intuitive appreciation of her feelings, Tania felt burningly embarrassed that James would have discussed their private affairs with this man. It antagonised her towards him even more. She didn't want to feel exposed to his understanding. She didn't want anything from him.

She opened her mouth to give him some blisteringly witty remark that would leave him in no doubt of her resentment, when those dark eyes of his, that she could only describe as hot and intense, held her own in a penetrating look.

"You and James were twins, weren't you? I wouldn't have thought so. You look younger than twenty-four." His gaze scanned her face, as if he could see into her very pores. Tania squirmed under so frank a gaze, feeling the delicate colour stain her cheeks once more.

"You caught me at a bad moment," she said crisply. "Just out of the bath and with no make-up on, no woman looks her best— "

"I didn't say that you didn't look good, Tania," the voice was more seductive when it softened. "You have a beautiful skin texture. It would be a crime to hide it with make-up. You don't need to enhance your bone structure, nor to prove that you're a woman. That fact is very obvious to me."

He didn't actually undress her with his eyes, nor even move his gaze any lower than her neck, but the effect on her was the same as if he had physically slipped the

12

Chinese robe from her shoulders. Tania could almost feel the coolness of the air against her flesh as the unbidden fantasy of it filled every part of her. She shivered. It was as if she heard James's eager young voice in her head, drumming the words at her again. This time, when he had contacted her after he and Claude had struck up their friendship.

"He's the best, Tania. An expert on the mountains, and the finest teacher any novice could want. He's also the most charismatic man for miles around. It's a good thing it's me and not you who's taking on the Lundgard climb with him next weekend. You'd go all besotted over the man, like all the other women around here!"

Tania didn't want the image of James to be so strong in her mind tonight. The day itself had been ordeal enough, without Claude Girard managing to conjure up some of the poignant moments she and James had shared. She certainly didn't want James's posthumous reminder that Claude Girard was charismatic . . . she could see that well enough for herself.

"You have the same extraordinary eyes as James," Claude said, still watching her. "On him, they were tigerish, showing his keen enthusiasm for some of the gruelling tasks we undertook on the mountains."

She was willing to admit that there were rescues too, as well as what Tania called the reckless clambering about on rocks! James and Claude had formed a superb mountain rescue team, and had been duly honoured in various parts of the world because of it.

"Cat's eyes, James used to call mine," Tania said abruptly. She had finished her meal, and her fingers reached for a bread roll, merely to give them something to do. Claude's hand covered hers across the table. Beneath

13

his touch, she felt trapped, as if her whole body was held in the gentle grip of those strong male fingers. I must be going mad, Tania thought angrily. She snatched her hand away, biting into the bread roll without tasting it. Her heartbeats were erratic.

Claude laughed, a rich, husky sound. "Then he had no soul, Tania. Your eyes are beautiful, like warm honey— "

She couldn't take any more of this. She put down the bread roll and looked directly into his eyes. "You didn't come all this way just to flatter me, Claude. You got my letter. You know my feelings about the mountains, and you know I snubbed you by not wanting you at James's old college today. So either you're a masochist for coming here like this, or there's some other reason, and I want to know what it is. Just what do you want?"

"I want you," he stated. No more, no less. He returned her stare unflinchingly, daring her to read what she would into his statement. Tania flushed an angry red. At this rate, she'd end up lobster-hued, she thought!

"You'd better explain that remark," she said freezingly. Far from putting him off, she was annoyed to see it amused him. He threw back his head and laughed again. She could see why he was so attractive to women, physically at least. He had a strong face, very tanned from the outdoor life he led. Strong and masculine, and yet somehow he gave out such an aura of sensitivity that a woman felt instantly aware that he would be a tender and considerate lover. Tania hated herself, as well as Claude, for even letting the thought into her head for a single moment.

"My dear, lovely Tania, forgive me! I didn't mean to shock you, but your prim English reaction was so like the way James described you— "

"Did he?" She forgot her antagonism for a moment as his words checked her thoughts. "I don't think I was ever prim."

"I'm very glad to hear it." There was a definite grin on Claude's face now. "And I didn't mean to imply that James gave me a strait-laced idea of you, merely that you disapproved of his choice of career, and to him you were always the cautious one. Afraid of shadows, I believed he phrased it."

"Charming! I'm not sure I like to think you discussed me on your day trips!" She minimised the danger of their work in a kind of self-defence. Claude's eyes glinted, but he made no comment.

"Oh, we sometimes had other things to think about," he assured her lightly. "But to clarify my earlier statement, I'll try to be as brief as possible."

"That would be best. I have a friend coming to see me this evening," Tania said pointedly, half-hoping that David would turn up after all and put an end to this ridiculous confrontation.

Claude ignored the barb. "I have been approached by a French publisher who wants me to write a book about James and me, and I need your help. We want to use a different angle from the usual thing of recent exploits leading to James's tragic death, and where do I go on from here, kind of thing. Our backgrounds are very different. Mine was quite well-to-do and pampered. James's was – well – you know it better than I, and that's where you come in. I want to compare those early years, describing our backgrounds and seeing what turned us into the men we became. Socially from vastly different lives, yet ultimately with the same ideals and incentives. I gather your parents worked on a shoestring until they were rewarded for their researches, enabling them to send you and James to the schools they wanted for you. But my information is all very sketchy.'' He paused for breath.

Tania's own breathing had quickened. "Why should I help you? Why should I exploit something in which I knew only fear for my brother? Fear which was well founded as it turned out. Why should I help you write a book to make money, and lead some other poor unfortunate enthusiasts to kill themselves— '' She was winding herself up very effectively.

"Because if you don't – and the book isn't all that I want it to be, a tribute to James as well as an account of our failures and our triumphs – then it will be as if he never lived. As if you're giving yourself the right to deny his very existence. Do you think you have that right, Tania? Is that how James would have wanted you to react to my suggestion, or would he say you were being afraid of shadows again?''

She felt the damp beads of perspiration on her skin. This wasn't fair . . . it wasn't fair . . .

'That's emotional blackmail,'' she whispered, her voice shaking. "How dare you use my love for my brother to get what you want? I don't need to see his life portrayed in a book to keep his memory alive. It's all here, in my heart.''

She pressed her hand against the silk robe, feeling the taut nipple beneath her fingers, not because of any sexual arousal, but because her hatred of Claude Girard's methods had tightened her whole body. She loathed him, and he had no right to come here with his cleverly worded suggestions. It didn't help her equilibrium to see his eyes stray to where she clutched at herself. Her hand dropped away at once.

"Are you so selfish that you want to keep his memory all to yourself, Tania?" Claude went on relentlessly. "Other people loved him too, and respected him and admired him. James wanted the story told. We had talked about it vaguely from time to time, and when the publisher wrote to me, it was as if James was prodding me from somewhere in the ether. Telling me this was the time."

It was too much like her own weird feelings that James was somewhere around, approving all this. If she hadn't felt so emotionally involved, Tania would have scoffed at the idea. And if James had any crazy ideas that he could do a little matchmaking between his sister and his partner, he could forget it! She passed the back of her hand across her forehead. Was she going completely crazy, to be thinking like that!

As if realising that Tania was unable to think clearly any longer, Clause stood up, towering over her at the table.

"You'll need time to consider, of course. I have to tell you that I am going ahead with the book in any case. Naturally I hope for your co-operation. There is always the danger of half-truths creeping in, unless facts are verified, and I would hate to do James a disservice in that way."

Oh, but he was so clever, she thought furiously. He was blackmailing her to agree as surely as if he held a gun to her head. Knowing she couldn't run the risk of her brother's memory being falsified in any way. She rose and walked past him towards the door, her chin high. Her hair seemed to cling damply to her neck. She felt as if she had covered a hundred years in one short hour of knowing Claude Girard.

"I'll think about it."

"Of course. I'll call you tomorrow afternoon. I'm

staying in London for the weekend." He came towards her, and she avoided looking at him, afraid he would see the active dislike in her eyes. Her hand reached for the door handle to wrench it open, but before she could reach it, he had caught her arm in an iron grip and pulled her into his arms. Tania gasped with fury and outrage, struggling vainly to free herself, and then his words made her pause just a little. They were spoken very close to her face, his breath warm on her cheek.

"You know the circumstances of James's accident," he said in a low voice. "The terrible fall, the dreadful injuries. He was alive when we reached him, but barely conscious. It was a relief to us all when he blacked out."

She swallowed, the imagery he evoked too painful for comfort. Why was he doing this . . . ?

"James was one of the bravest men I ever knew," Claude went on. "And although you may have washed your hands of him, he was always very proud of you. The clever one of the family, James said. You never knew him as I did, Tania, despite your blood ties. You never fought to survive the elements with him. That's when you really learn a man's worth. You know him to his soul and beyond. That's why I knew he would have wanted me to contact you."

Tania's mouth was dry, hardly knowing how to answer this. There was a tremor in Claude's deep voice, betraying his own emotion, signifying the truth of his words. She could feel its resonance against her body where his chest crushed her breasts, as he would crush her to his will. His eyes slowly focused on her face, and she held her breath at the look.

"The last words I ever heard James say, referred to you," Claude said. "He was jaunty, even to the end, even though I had difficulty in picking up the words."

He dangled the bait, and she couldn't resist. She had to know. "What did he say?" she whispered.

After the briefest pause he told her.

"Kiss Tania for me."

Even as she registered the words, Claude Girard was putting the words into action. Her lips were still slightly parted when she felt the pressure of his strong, sensual mouth touching hers. Gently at first, and then with a ruthless, crushing passion, his fingers tangling in her hair. As if he was driven on by a promise to his dead companion, the kiss seemed to go on endlessly, holding Tania bemused as if she was in some fantasy world. A stranger had stormed into her life and was kissing her as if he owned her . . . she struggled out of his arms, but before she could tell him just what she thought of him, he had turned on his heel and walked out of the flat without another word.

Chapter 2

Tania couldn't have said whether she stood there for minutes or hours. She seemed to be transfixed to the spot where Claude Girard had left her, while some of the worst adjectives she could think of to describe him raged through her mind – and in several languages at that. He was arrogant, despicable, a blatant womaniser, shamelessly using her love for James to get what he wanted . . . those were only the mild things she thought about Claude Girard. She scrubbed her hand across her mouth, still tasting his kiss. Once he had left the room, it was still filled with him . . . he dominated her senses, whether she wanted him to or not. She despised him. She didn't dare question whether or not James's last-heard words to him were true. She wanted them to be, because of James, not because of the man who delivered them as James had wished.

She was still standing motionless, with every nerve-end alive and tingling, when the sound of the doorbell right alongside her made her jump. If he had come back again, he could stand there for ever, she thought furiously. They had nothing more to say to one another.

"Go away," she shouted at the door. "You've done enough for one evening!"

"Tania, it's me!" David's anxious voice came through the wood panelling. "Are you all right?"

She opened the door with trembling hands, almost dragging him inside. He was as tall as Claude Girard, nearly as dark, but without the indefinable Continental charm . . . Tania's full mouth twisted. Oh yes, Claude had charm all right, but it wasn't the sort that appealed to her. For one thing, she didn't feel the need to drag the Chinese robe more firmly around her body when David was around, the way she had with Claude. Its lines were perfectly respectable, but she had still felt at a distinct disadvantage when the Frenchman was around.

"What's going on, Tania?" David Lee said at once. He took in the table still set with two places, and the remains of a meal. She couldn't blame him for the speculative look in his eyes then, considering her appearance.

She didn't owe him any explanations. He didn't own her . . . The same phrase she'd used about Claude's assault on her senses slipped into her mind. Somehow it sounded far more harmless when used in David's case. But maybe she did owe him something. He was her friend, while she could never think of Claude Girard as anything but her enemy.

"An unexpected visitor, that's all," she tried to make her voice light, and only succeeded in sounding husky. "I'm sorry I yelled at you, David. It hasn't been a good day."

He put a sympathetic arm around her shoulders, squeezing the soft silk of her robe. She didn't feel any need to flinch away. With David, she felt very little, if she was honest, just a comfortable friendship. He should find some nice girl to marry and raise a family, she sometimes thought. There was no point in him hanging around her, because their relationship was never going anywhere beyond this point. But since he was here,

21

she leaned on him, physically and mentally, at that moment.

"I thought it would be rough on you, going to your brother's old college, love. I would have taken you if you'd asked. I could have taken the time off— "

The ceremony at the college seemed light years away. The tension of the occasion had been nothing compared with Claude Girard's arrival in London and into her life. She couldn't rid her thoughts of him now. She realised she was going off into a dream world when David stopped talking and looked down at her, frowning.

"You look as if you need a drop of brandy, Tania. You were quite flushed when I came in, but you've gone very white now. Sit down, and I'll fetch you some. I know where it is."

She obeyed like a rag doll. It was a fair description of how she felt. It was just as if she had glimpsed a little of the future in those split seconds, and seen that her life was destined to be inextricably bound up with Claude Girard's. As if some quirk of fate had ordained that with James gone, she was to slip into his role of companion to Claude. The uncanny feeling washed over her and made her shiver. She wasn't normally given to second sight, nor even sure that she believed in it, but the feeling was so strong that she clutched at the glass of brandy David handed her and swallowed it down, praying that its sting would enable her to laugh at such fanciful thoughts. In reality, she knew she was perilously near to crying. The college business, and the talk with Claude Girard, had brought James vividly near, reviving all the anguish of six months ago, when she had learned of his death on a French mountain.

"Better now?" David still peered at her anxiously.

Slightly short-sighted without his trendy glasses he used at the office, it gave him an endearingly caring look. Any woman would feel cherished, married to David. Tania moved restlessly, hardly knowing why such thoughts kept coming into her head, when she had no intention of being his wife.

"I'm fine, really," she smiled into his face. The brandy must be doing its work, from the warm glow spreading through her. It was calming her nerves a little anyway. "I'm sorry I gave you a fright, David. The last person in the world I wanted to see turned up here tonight, and it threw me, that's all."

"Not Claude Girard?" With great forbearance, he stopped himself asking how it was she gave him a meal, when he knew very well how much she detested him and all he stood for. It was a trait that was alternately well-bred and irritating, to Tania's thinking. Any other red-blooded male would have demanded to know who had been sharing her table that night . . . and jealously wondered if he had shared anything else.

Then she realised immediately that there was a charge of excitement in David's eyes.

"I thought he looked familiar. I was puzzling who the man was that I saw leaving the front of the building in a taxi as I came in. Of course, Claude Girard, the mountaineer. I had hoped to get a glimpse of him this afternoon, but I missed him."

"This afternoon?" Like an echo, Tania repeated the words, while a slow, ominous premonition ran through her. She had been safely away at James's old college. David Lee worked at the same company where she was a linguist on contract.

"He was at the office." David confirmed her worst

23

fears. "I didn't get the chance to ask Lance what he was doing there, but we assumed it might be something to do with you. I thought he may have turned up at the college, and I knew you'd have hated that. He didn't, I suppose?"

Tania was seething. Why was Claude Girard checking up on her? The company she worked for dealt in machine parts for aeroplanes. There was nothing of interest there for a mountaineer. Nothing except herself, when the mountaineer in question was Claude Girard. She made an instant decision.

"Will you drive me round to Lance's place, David? I can be dressed in five minutes. Make yourself some coffee while you're waiting if you like. I've got to find out what this is all about."

"Don't you know?" His voice followed her to the bedroom. "What did he come here for? What did he want?"

I want you!

Tania seemed to hear Claude's words floating around in her head, giving them a meaning that was all too clear. Whatever his initial reason for coming here – the book on which he was working – there had been a smouldering sexuality in the arrogant words and mouth. Claude Girard was a man of strong passions and a ruthless determination. James had once told her that. Tania had blocked out the memory from her mind while she was verbally sparring with Claude, but now she also remembered something else James had said to her in his admiration of the other man, only six years his senior, yet far more mature in every way than Tania's brother.

"He feels a crazy need to conquer every mountain, Tania. To own them, as a man owns a woman— "

24

"Men don't own women," she had replied. "That's medieval."

"According to Claude, every man desires one woman so fiercely that every primitive urge in him is aroused. He has a strange way of communicating, sometimes, and maybe Claude is a little medieval in his thinking. He certainly has a powerful influence over everyone he meets."

The suddenly memory of those dark smouldering eyes, attempting to persuade her to agree to his suggestion by his very will, made Tania shudder, as she pulled a thin sweater over her head and zipped up her cotton slacks. David was dressed casually, and had obviously expected to take her to a favourite riverside pub that evening. Lance Hillman, the managing director of the company, lived with his wife and family near by. He wouldn't object to Tania and David dropping in for half an hour, especially when it was something so important to her peace of mind.

"Well?" David's voice interrupted her flow of thought, as she came out of the bedroom. "What did Claude Girard want?"

"He wants me to co-operate with him on some book he's been commissioned to do, about himself and James. He wants me to supply the background information on James's life."

"Sounds terrific. It would be nice for James to be remembered in that way," David nodded, not seeing. Tania felt frustration creep over her. Did all men club together in some strange clannish manner that excluded women whenever it suited them?

"No, it wouldn't," she said, nettled. "Not for me, anyway."

They left the flat and walked around the block to where

David's car was parked in a side road. He looked at her in astonishment.

"Don't you think James deserves to be honoured for posterity?"

He talked the way Claude had talked. Playing on her emotions, setting her up as the fall guy. Tania could cheerfully have throttled the whole male population of the world at that moment.

"I just don't want to be involved with Claude Girard, that's all." She avoided a straight answer. "And I've a feeling I'm not going to be too pleased when I know why he went to see Lance today."

She discovered that that was an understatement. An hour later, when the car had threaded its way through the London traffic and was out on the less congested roads leading to the pleasant green-belt houses of the suburbs, Tania's heart was thumping as they pulled up at Lance's tree-shaded home.

His wife, Josie, welcomed them in with a pleased smile, saying it was ages since she had seen Tania, and offering them both a drink. Lance greeted them just as affably, though Tania knew him well enough to see the look of caution in his eyes. Stocky and middle aged, he still had the guilty look of a schoolboy caught stealing apples when he had anything to hide.

"You know why I've come, don't you, Lance?" she said at once, with the directness for which she was noted. He shifted his gaze slightly.

"Should I?" he countered.

"Claude Girard. Do I have to spell it out for you, or are you going to tell me why he went to see you today of all days, when he knew very well I'd be out of the way?"

"He could have come to see me on a matter that doesn't concern you," Lance hedged.

Tania gave a snort. "Come on, Lance. I'm not leaving here until you tell me!"

The managing director gave a rueful grin at his wife. "You see how my staff treat me? There's no respect these days. Young people used to doff their caps to their elders— "

"I'll doff you one if you don't tell me!" Tania didn't feel like playing games. If Josie thought she was being rude, then Tania would apologise later. But Josie was becoming just as impatient with her husband as Tania, as if some womanly intuition told her how important this was to the other woman.

"All right." Lance gave in. "Claude Girard very persuasively and charmingly got me to agree to release you from your contract for the next six months so that you can go to France with him to collaborate on the book he's writing. Since it deals in depth with your brother, he put it very delicately that he knew you would want to help him. The man should have been a diplomat."

"What!" Tania jumped to her feet, spilling sherry down her slacks, her eyes blazing. Every nerve in her body was vibrating with anger at the audacity of the man. Going behind her back like that and enlisting Lance's support before he had even spoken to her was nothing short of insulting. How dare he override her wishes like this! It was obvious that he'd expected the reaction he had got from her. Did he really think this underhand method was going to change anything?

"You didn't agree to it, surely?" Tania spluttered. "Not without consulting me first?"

27

"Now then, my dear, of course I didn't. Not entirely, anyway," Lance said uneasily.

"And just what does that mean?" she demanded.

Lance shrugged. "I couldn't let you off the payroll for six months just like that, Tania, and I told the man as much. Naturally I assumed he'd already discussed all this with you, and was putting his own case to me in case you felt embarrassed at requesting six months' leave."

"No, he hadn't discussed it with me," she said angrily. "And since when have I been unable to speak for myself?"

"In half a dozen different languages," David put in flippantly, trying to lighten the atmosphere. Tania didn't even bother to glare at him.

"You didn't agree to it, did you, Lance?" Her voice was shriller than usual. He couldn't have done. The company couldn't spare her, and they'd never pay her for a six-month absence, if that was what Girard had in mind. They certainly wouldn't give her six months' unpaid leave while she flitted about Europe, for whatever reason.

Lance looked at her uneasily. Those amber eyes of hers could really spit fire when they chose to, he thought, and right now their fury was all directed at him. There was more than a little truth in the old cliché about a woman being beautiful when she was angry . . . but he knew better than to try complimenting Tania Paget with any soft platitudes at that moment.

"Tania, believe me, I assumed the man had talked it all over with you. He was so plausible, so sure of himself." At Tania's bitter look, he spread his hands helplessly. "Hell, Tania, I'm only human! I know you never had a good word to say about him at one time, but lately you never even mention his name. And Girard talked as if you and he had something going. How was I to know any different? He spoke as if you were just dying to get to France with him. When he told me he was willing to pay the company for hiring a temporary linguist for the six months so that your job would be assured if and when you wanted it back, well, I— "

"He *what*?" Tania couldn't believe what he was saying. "Claude Girard went to you and offered to buy me out for six months? He offered to *buy* me?"

For someone normally so eloquent, words were beginning to fail her. All she could feel was a raging fury at the man she loathed for putting her in this situation. Did he think he was God, to manipulate her any way he wanted? Did he really think he was that strong, that powerful? And did he really think her so weak that she would agree so readily? If so, he had a shock coming to him, and the light of battle glinted like fire in her expressive eyes.

"Tania, love, don't get yourself all worked up," Josie was saying gently. "I'm sure there's a way around this, and Lance only did what he thought you wanted. No harm's been done yet, has it? This Girard put the idea forward to Lance, but it can just as quickly be rejected. Don't let it spoil your lovely evening with David."

Josie's forte was soothing troubled waters. With two rebellious teenage sons she was well used to it, and Tania's little storm did nothing to ruffle Josie's calm surface. Tania gave her a quick, apologetic hug.

"All right. I'm sorry for upsetting your weekend, Josie, but I had to find out what was going on." Her voice was jerky with embarrassment. Josie smiled reassuringly.

"You haven't spoiled anything here, Tania. We're used

29

to sparks flying in this house. You talk to Lance in the office on Monday and get things sorted out."

Lance might be boss of the company, but Josie smoothed things out at home, Tania realised. He looked relieved as the small, slight woman took command, and five minutes later, Tania and David were driving the short distance to the riverside pub they favoured. She still bristled inside, but as Josie said, no real harm had been done. If anything, Claude Girard had done her a favour, because now she knew just how ruthless a man he was. The kind of man a woman would do well to keep away from. David eyed her thoughtfully as they sat in the soft blue darkness of the pub garden, the fairy-lights reflected in the rippling flow of the river like miniature rainbows.

"You know, there's one thing to say for all this business with the Frenchman, Tania," he remarked. "I haven't seen you so alive for a long time. You haven't exactly been wallowing in misery since your brother's death, at least, not so that anyone could see, but you haven't been as animated as you used to be either. Tonight, you seem to have got the old sparkle back, even if it's only anger that's doing it!"

"Thanks," she said tartly, not wanting to admit that he could be right. Not wanting to admit, even to herself, that despite her hatred of him, Claude Girard acted like a stimulant to her senses, that was at once heady and dangerous.

Tania was ready for Claude's phone call the next day. All afternoon she waited impatiently, intending to give him a piece of her mind at what he had done. She hadn't slept because of him. Instead, she had drifted off into fitful, restless dreams where she was falling, falling, much as

James must have fallen, with nothing but space and air beneath her. The wind rushed past her body, and always at the last minute before she plunged off the edge of space, strong hands would be there to save her, to hold her and comfort her, and a voice would be whispering her name over and over, speaking of destiny and love, and she would be wide awake in an instant, her body tangled in the bed-clothes, drenched in perspiration. After a sleepless night, she felt she knew the touch of Claude Girard's hands as well as she knew her own, and it was something she didn't want to know at all.

By four o'clock she decided he wasn't going to phone. He was doing this deliberately, Tania thought furiously, keeping her on a string. If it rang now, she damn well wouldn't answer it . . .

When it did, she snatched up the receiver, trying not to notice the way her heart pounded.

"I'm sorry it's so late," Claude's rich voice said in her ear, his accent more pronounced over the phone. "I've had things to do all day. I'll pick you up about seven thirty. I've booked a table for us for dinner. Don't keep me waiting."

The line went dead before she could say a single word. Tania looked at it stupidly, unbelievably. How could she have been so railroaded? She was normally well in command of any situation. It was part of her job, especially when uncertain foreigners at business meetings looked to her to smooth the way for them. Claude Girard wasn't going to storm into her life like this.

The easy way was to be out when he called for her that evening. She could go to the cinema, a theatre. She could phone a girlfriend, or David, and simply not be there to answer the doorbell. But for all that James once said

31

she was afraid of shadows, Tania wasn't one to shirk a head-on confrontation with someone. It was the second time she had thought of her meeting with Claude in those terms, but that was how she saw it. There was nothing conventional in their meeting. There never could be.

She felt a sudden annoyance at Claude's assumption that she was the timid twin. She had a responsible job, which she enjoyed, among people she liked. If it sounded deadly dull compared with the flamboyant lifestyle of Claude and her brother, and the celebrity world in which he apparently moved whenever he conquered another mountain, then it was just too bad. It was her life.

All the same, Tania had no wish to appear the little country cousin at dinner that evening. She would show him she was a city girl, used to the sophisticated London nightlife . . . even if she only indulged in it infrequently. There was no need for him to know that! She chose her clothes and make-up with care, and had the satisfaction of seeing his dark eyes widen slightly when he called for her.

He looked her over slowly, from the swathed hair around her head with the enticing tendrils to soften the line, to the stunning gold eye make-up that emphasised her eyes, to the luscious pink-gold lipstick. His eyes moved farther down, to the sleek black cocktail dress threaded with silver, and the high-heeled shoes and velvet evening bag.

"So. The little duckling of yesterday is in reality a beautiful swan!" Claude murmured with old-fashioned charm. She had hardly noticed what he carried in his hand, she was too taken up with his own appearance, elegantly tall in a dark suit and dazzling white shirt that hadn't been picked up in a chainstore. His whole aura was expensive, and while she was still digesting the fact, she became aware of those hands she remembered so well from her restless dreams.

They brushed against her breast, and a small breath caught in her throat as she felt its quick response. Then she realised he was fastening a small corsage from a florist's box on to her dress, and the Continental gesture was unexpected and charming. When he had fastened them securely, the scent of the pink rosebuds drifted into her nostrils, and he let one finger trail against the smooth skin of her throat before he stood back to admire her.

"Now you have the finishing touch," Claude murmured, and Tania wasn't sure whether he referred to the corsage or his own feathery fingering of her skin at that moment. His touch seemed to electrify her. Minutes later, she could still feel the contact his skin had made with hers.

The anger of last night, when she had discovered that Claude had been to see Lance Hillman still simmered inside her, ready to explode. She had intended waiting until after dinner before she told him just what she thought of him. He may as well feed her . . . but his undoubted sexual assault on her sent the anger flaring once again. She moved back a pace from him, her mouth tightening.

"Well, now that you've realised I'm not a little duckling," Tania flashed at him, "perhaps you'll also realise I'm not the type of woman to be manipulated to whatever the great Claude Girard wants."

His dark eyes narrowed. He hadn't expected this. Tania could see now that he fully intended to exploit his male animal appeal to get what he wanted. He'd soon learn that it wouldn't work with her, she thought keenly.

"I merely want to escort a beautiful woman to dinner,"

his voice was mild, but she could hear the steely thread beneath the calm. "What Frenchman would choose to be alone on a warm London evening, when he can have a lovely woman at his side?"

This kind of seduction left her cold. Tania told herself so, refusing to admit that her heart was racing and that it was not entirely due to anger. She remembered last night.

"I didn't ask you to come here. Whatever your motives, I would have preferred not to have met you. I thought I'd made that very clear. As for what you did yesterday while I was at James's old college – " Her voice trembled a little. She could still hardly believe that he could have had the audacity to try and buy her time from the company the way he had.

"Ah." Claude clearly saw that she knew it all now. He showed no sign of shame or remorse, Tania raged. "Then you will know there is no problem with your employer. You will come to my home and work on the book with me, as I wish, and as James would have wished. Then, when the work is done, you may resume your old life – if you still want to."

Tania stared at him. She barely heard what he said. It was the sheer self-confidence of the man that left her almost speechless. Almost . . .

"You're not listening to me, are you, Claude?" she raged at him. "I've no intention of working on anything with you. I have a life of my own. I'm happy with it. It's what I chose, and the last thing I want is to get any closer to something that only brought me pain and unhappiness."

"Do you always run away from things?"

She stared at him helplessly. They seemed to have cut

across the barrier of conventionality frighteningly fast. He questioned her in a way David Lee would never dare to do, after knowing her for two years. Time seemed to have no meaning where Tania and Claude were concerned. In some strange way she felt as if she had known him always. Probably because of the snippets of information James had told her about him, and the occasional newspaper cutting. And yet, she really knew very little about him if she thought about it. Only his career and his undoubted attraction for women, and the fact that he and James had made a great team in all their undertakings. Personally, he was a closed book – and she intended keeping it that way. Claude had very different intentions.

"Do you always act this way with strangers?" Tania countered, her face beginning to feel heated again. A small smile touched his mouth. She found herself looking at it, seeing the way his lips curved, revealing regular teeth and an oddly tender expression. His hand reached out towards her again, and one finger followed the contour of her cheek as if he wanted to learn its shape by heart.

"You and I were never strangers, Tania," he said softly. "I know too much about you from James. Our families were frequent topics of conversation while we rested from a climb in a cold canvas tent on a mountainside."

The thought of it made her shiver. "You do have a family then?" She asked sarcastically. "I thought you were too much the loner to have any encumbrances."

To her surprise, a look of something like pain shot across his face. It took Tania an instant to register it, and then it was gone so fast she wondered if she had imagined it.

"I have a family," he stated without expression. "I'll tell you about them over dinner. We *are* having dinner tonight, I suppose? Or have you got all dressed up like this just to tease me?"

"I've no intention of teasing you," she said quickly.

"Good. Then since the taxi's been waiting outside with its meter ticking away, I suggest we go."

She followed him out of the flat and into the taxi. He gave the driver the name of a swish hotel, and half an hour later they were sitting together in a discreet little alcove with silent waiters ready to do their bidding. Claude certainly lived up to his image, Tania thought caustically.

They ordered their meal and a bottle of wine, and it was all served to them with perfection. Succulent steaks and a frothy sweet concoction to follow would put on pounds in weight, Tania thought, but it was all too good to resist. Besides, a few extra pounds wouldn't hurt her.

"You were going to tell me about your family," she prompted, when they were drinking coffee and liqueurs. She imagined that he lived in some elegant bachelor establishment, though she vaguely remembered hearing some reference to a family home in the south of France. James may have told her something, but she'd never really wanted to know. Or she may have read something in an article . . .

"I live at my family home, south of Bordeaux," Claude said. "I have my own quarters there— "

"Quarters? You make it sound like an army barracks!"

Claude laughed. "Not quite! Though it's probably big enough for that. No, it's just that I have my study for my work, and my own rooms for when I want to entertain my friends. It's more convenient for me and the rest of the household."

"I see." What Tania saw was the indulged son of the house. What his "entertaining" amounted to, she didn't care to know. It wasn't her business.

"I don't think you do, *chérie*." The French endearment made her heart leap a little. "But no matter. You'll understand when you come to France."

"I've already told you I'm not going!" she said heatedly.

"Not even for James?" The emotional blackmail was there again, but this time his eyes challenged hers, knowing that by now she would have thought about it, considered it. There was no doubt in his mind that she would accept. She could see it as clearly as if it was written all over him.

"I suppose you're waited on hand and foot in this huge mausoleum of yours," she mocked him, ignoring his words.

"We have staff, yes. Of course. It's necessary." He spoke with such acceptance of what was to him a normal way of life that Tania felt a little ashamed of her comment. Trying to amend matters would probably make it worse, and in any case, Claude was searching in his wallet for some snapshots.

"This is my mother." He showed her a photo of a silver-haired lady of obvious wealth. Uneasily, Tania remembered James's one-time comment that even if the rest of the world thought Claude Girard a playboy, those who knew him well could tell differently. "And this is my sister, Monique. She lives with us at the château now, since her husband died— "

"The château?" Tania echoed. James had definitely never mentioned any château! Communication between herself and her brother had been strained in the past year or so, and she had thought the idea of James and Claude starting the mountain rescue team was even more foolhardy than the sponsored climbs on precipitous slopes.

Claude pushed another photo under her nose. "And this is Henri." His voice had perceptibly changed, in a way Tania couldn't quite define. It had roughened slightly, yet was infinitely caring, and her heart lurched as she looked at the photo of the small boy with laughing dark eyes and tousled dark hair. He was the image of Claude. The boy smiled into the camera from a child-size wheelchair. Tania stared at it, not quite knowing what to say.

"I'd give him the mountains if I could," Claude said, a subdued, vibrant anger in his tone.

Tania passed her tongue over her dry lips. Who was Henri . . . ?

As if he sensed the unspoken question, Claude looked up at her from the snapshot. "Henri is Monique's son, my nephew. He's eight years old, and highly intelligent. He loves the mountains, and knows nearly as much about them as I do – though purely theoretically, of course. He's trapped inside that damned wheelchair."

Abruptly, he put the photos away, and Tania knew at once that this was Claude's vulnerable area. She hadn't believed he had one, until now. It was obvious that he loved the child dearly, and bitterly resented whatever it was that had put him in the wheelchair. Claude was the enemy, but at that moment it was she who felt like reaching out and touching his hand . . . She didn't. Instead, she asked very quietly if he wanted to tell her about it.

"Another time. We'll have some more coffee and another drink and then I'll take you home. You have plenty to think about, and I'll be in touch again tomorrow. Perhaps we could go walking in Hyde Park. I'm told it's something every foreign visitor is supposed to do when he comes to London, and on the few occasions I've been here, I've never found the time for it. Shall I call for you after lunch?"

It never entered Tania's mind to say no. So smoothly she hardly knew how it was happening, Claude Girard was slowly taking over her life. It was only for this one weekend, she told herself later, as she prepared for bed, with the memory of the chaste kiss he had pressed to her lips as they parted. This one weekend, and then she would never see him again.

The thought was not quite as satisfying as she had expected. There were facets of the man she had never imagined before. He wasn't as totally brash or devil-may-care as she had thought. The playboy image seemed to disperse a little when she recalled that haunted look on his face when he gazed at the photo of his small nephew. It was a look that haunted Tania too as she wondered if she was in for another sleepless night on account of Claude Girard.

Her last drifting thought as she finally encountered sleep, was that it might settle her nerves more quickly if she did as he wanted and went to France with him. Perhaps she did owe it to James . . . the images of her brother and Claude and the handicapped Henri became all jumbled in her mind before blackness eventually blotted them all out.

Chapter 3

"You must see that I can't possibly stay for six months," Tania said firmly, as she and Claude sat on a park bench the following afternoon. The day was hot, and she wore a thin summer dress and ropey sandals. Claude's arm slid along her back, and she edged away a little. She had no wish to resemble any of the other dozens of couples out for a Sunday afternoon in Hyde Park. Lovers, most of them . . . and Claude was anything but her lover!

"Why not?" Claude said immediately. "I'm not a writer, and I'll need time to work on the book. You've got more insight into setting out reports and so on than I, so your help in that area will be invaluable as well as the information on James that I need, *chérie*.'

She looked at him suspiciously. "Claude, I have a job. I'm coming back to it. I don't want to stay any longer than necessary." She spoke deliberately, as if she spoke to a child, although he was anything but that. He leaned towards her, his thigh warm against her own in the beige linen slacks he wore. His face was close to hers, but no-one noticed them, or cared. To anyone else, they were just two more lovers enjoying a day out . . .

She wished these stupid thoughts didn't keep coming into her mind! She was suddenly very conscious of him as a man. A very sensual man who, whether she liked it

40

or not, had the power to completely reverse her strongest intentions. No man should have that much power over another person.

"Tania, if I could, I would keep you in my château for ever, but I give you my word you'll be free to leave whenever you wish. I'm not your jailor."

Not physically, maybe. But right then he was holding her captive with the very power of his personality. His arm had tightened around her shoulder, and she could feel its warmth through her thin dress. His other hand had somehow moved to rest lightly on her leg above her knee, and she could feel the pressure of his fingers there. He seemed to dominate her whole being, belying his own words. She was imprisoned by him at that moment as surely as Henri was chained to his wheelchair.

Remembering the boy, Tania shifted away from Claude. All right. Somehow – Lord knew how – she had agreed to do as Claude wanted and go to France with him, but for as short a time as possible. She still seethed when she thought of how he had gone to Lance and prepared the way . . . but it was now a *fait accompli*, and she wouldn't go back on her word.

"You said you would tell me about Henri," she said hesitantly, remembering too the closed-in look of pain on Claude's face on the previous evening. "If you'd rather not— "

He shook his head quickly. "It's best that you know before you meet him. It happened several years ago before his father died. The family all lived near Paris then, and Henri was an athletic little boy, the pride of his parents and the rest of his family. He always wanted to climb a mountain with me someday. I told him he would. I promised him."

Tania felt her throat thicken. It was clearly abhorrent to Claude that it was a promise that couldn't be kept.

"His father had taken him riding in the Bois de Boulogne in Paris. A car backfired and frightened Henri's pony. It bolted and threw him. His foot was still caught in the stirrup and he was dragged along the ground for some distance." Claude's voice had become heavy and strained as he relived the moments. "At first we thought he was only badly bruised. He wasn't even concussed. He spent a week in hospital being thoroughly checked over, and gradually we learned that it was far more than bruising. It was a spinal injury that prevents him from walking more than a very few laboured steps a day. The doctors say it may improve in time, or it may not."

Tania was horrified as she listened. "Can't they do anything for him?" Poor little boy, to be condemned to such a life.

"There's talk of some new operation, but it hasn't been perfected yet, and we've no wish for Henri to be used as a guinea-pig," he said, almost curtly. Tania guessed this question must have been the subject of some heart-rending discussions among the family. Her heart went out to them all at that moment. She put her hand on Claude's arm, pressing the hair-roughened skin beneath the pushed-up shirt sleeves.

"Saying that I'm sorry seems to be so inadequate," she murmured.

"Yes. We are all inadequate when fate steps in to shape our lives. You and I both know that, Tania. You lost a brother, and I a good friend and business colleague." He neatly turned the conversation away from the touchy subject so painful to him, and back to their own mutual concern. "I know that James would want us to be friends. I want that too."

She thought he was going to say something more, and she flinched away from any more maudlin references to her brother. The plain fact was that Claude had been closer to James in the past few years than she had been. It was no fault of either of them. It was simply that their lives hadn't touched after their parents died, and the brief affinity had flared and then died away. She could blame it on circumstances. Her parents' absorption in their own world, doing their best for their children, but inevitably depriving them of the home-life of normal children. Teaching them to be self-sufficient in their different ways, but denying them a lasting filial affection. Tania felt almost guilty at times, that the sadness she felt on account of James's death was more for all the lost years. Seeing how deeply Claude felt about his nephew's plight, and the fond affection with which he'd shown her his family snapshots last night, Tania was acutely conscious of the loss.

She felt guilty, too, that Claude might expect too much of her. Until now, she hadn't considered that what she had to tell him for his book might not be all that he expected. It was time he knew.

"Claude, I'm not sure how far back into James's life you mean to go with your book," she said quickly. "But although we spent all our time together until we were about Henri's age, we were both sent off to different schools then, and only saw each other at holiday times. Later, when our parents were financially able to do more for us, James went to college and I went to Paris. I don't want to come to France under false pretences."

She had the oddest feeling that he knew all that

43

already. James would have told him. So what did he want of her?

"You haven't answered my question," he stated.

"What question?"

He suddenly leaned forward and touched her lips with his mouth. His flesh was warm and firm. She could feel the tiny tingling sensations where the dark facial hair was already starting its regrowth by mid-afternoon. His masculine scent filled her nostrils. It was only a fleeting kiss, but after the previous emotional moments when she had realised his vulnerability, Tania had the strongest urge to wind her arms around his neck and pull him close. She resisted, the shock of her own reactions making her sharp as she repeated the words.

"I don't remember you asking me a question, Claude."

He laughed softly. "It was about our being friends. Only I'm not sure that friendship is quite what I have in mind. Perhaps we can discover a more delightful kind of relationship, you and I."

He ran his finger down her bare arm. The tiny golden hairs reacted shiveringly. She couldn't mistake the blatant meaning in his dark eyes. Memories of James telling her of Claude's conquests sharpened her voice even more.

"I wouldn't count on it. I have plenty of friends in England. I'm not looking for anything more."

"It sounds a very sterile kind of existence. No special man in your life, then?"

She wasn't falling into that trap. The next minute he'd tell her he was ready to fill the vacancy.

"Naturally I have a man friend. You only just missed him on Friday night as a matter of fact. I think I told you I was expecting someone."

She looked at him steadily, and saw the sudden speculation in his eyes. When he had arrived at Tania's flat, she had been dressed in the Chinese robe. If she had been expecting someone, a man, it was someone she knew very intimately. She could read his thoughts and stared him out boldly. Let him think what he liked. She wasn't getting entangled with Claude Girard, for all that he could stir her senses faster than any other man she had ever known. He was merely an episode in her life, not the whole book.

"He can't be such a special friend if he lets you spend the entire weekend with another man," Claude said abruptly.

Tania flushed. "You've hardly given me time to do anything else, have you? Anyway, David knows how I feel – felt – about you – " She could have bitten out her tongue as she altered the word to the past tense. Now Claude Girard would think she was adding herself to his list of conquests. But he didn't comment on it, except to say drily that he'd have to do his best to change her opinion of him, then.

Annoyed with herself, Tania knew that her opinion had already shifted gear a little. She didn't want to stop hating him and what he stood for, but the hatred wasn't such a deep shade of black as it had been two days ago. Was it really only two days ago that she had stood on the platform of James's old college and performed the little ceremony to open the sports hall in his name? Only two days ago that she met Claude Girard for the first time? It seemed as if she had always known him.

"When do you go back to France?" she asked quickly, wanting to change this conversation away from such personal probing.

"I intended going tomorrow, but I've decided to go tonight. So you're free to see your David this evening, if you want to . . ."

"Thank you!" Tania said sarcastically. It would be a long time before she asked his permission! The old antagonism was creeping up on her again. She welcomed it. It was safer than any growing warmth towards him.

"Can you be ready to fly to Bordeaux next Friday? I've cleared it with your managing director," Claude said calmly.

Her mouth dropped open. Lance hadn't said anything about dates, but there was no disputing the assurance in Claude's voice. If he said he'd cleared it with Lance, then he had.

"I don't know that I can— " she started to object.

"Don't mess me about, Tania. I've no time for prima donnas. You've agreed to come and I've fixed everything with your boss, so there's nothing to stop you. I'm giving you nearly a week to settle your affairs here. If this David is one of them, he'll have to learn to live without you for a while, so the sooner he starts, the better." Hard as the mountains now, Claude's voice told her he was tired of all the fencing about. Cold logic said he had every right to be. She *had* agreed, and there was no reason why next Friday shouldn't see her on her way to France. Almost dreamlike, she nodded, still wondering vaguely just how it had all happened, when it was the last thing she had intended.

David drove her to the airport during the late afternoon on Friday. He was quietly confident she would be back well within the six months the preposterous Claude Girard had arranged with Lance. His very complacency only made

Tania irritated with him. In David's eyes, Claude was a figure far removed from the norm. David was Mr Average, hard working, nice and attentive to women and babies, patient to the point of boredom at times . . .

Tania had never seen it so clearly before. She hadn't had the yardstick of Claude Girard to measure David's shortcomings by. It didn't endear her to Claude. Instead, it made her resent him even more for spoiling what she considered to be a perfect friendship with David, by showing up all his flaws. She clung to him at the airport, where everyone seemed to be kissing everyone else, and his arms held her close. She wished she could have felt something more than affection toward him, but she couldn't fall in love to order and David knew it.

"Write to me when you've got time," he said to her, a little huskily. "And don't let him become a slave-driver. I've met these types before. They play hard and work hard, and expect everyone else to run around in circles after them."

"Don't worry," Tania laughed. "I can take care of myself. I'll be back before you know it, David. You'll hardly have time to miss me!"

"I'll miss you," he assured her, and it was the nearest he came to showing any emotion. Tania's flight was called, and she walked away from him quickly. Whatever Claude might think of her relationship with David, she knew ruefully that it had always been a luke-warm one. Even David had never suspected that beneath the cool, efficient exterior she showed to the company, beat a deeply passionate heart, not yet fully awoken to her own sensuality. David Lee certainly hadn't been the one to awaken her.

The plane touched down after a smooth flight to

47

Bordeaux, and once through Customs and baggage claim, Tania's eyes sought and found a familiar figure standing at the barrier. Her heart leapt at the sight of Claude. He was the same man she had seen less than a week ago, and yet somehow, here in his own environment, he seemed larger, more forceful, attracting admiring eyes whenever he moved with that tall, lithe grace that distinguished him. He took her baggage from her hands and put it down a moment, then greeted her formally, kissing her lightly on both cheeks in the French fashion. The standard greeting to someone of more than a brief acquaintance, but who didn't qualify for being swept up into his arms and held dizzily to his heart . . .

Tania blinked, wondering if the thought had really surged into her mind. Even more, if the slight pang she felt was disappointment! She decided it was still the aftermath of seeing so many couples embracing at the London airport, and the same thing being enacted here. She didn't really want Claude Girard's arms around her, did she?

"The car's outside." Claude walked easily alongside her, the suitcases swinging in his hands, though to Tania they had weighed a ton. "Did you have a good journey? Not too bumpy? It can sometimes be a bit turbulent over the Channel."

"It was very smooth, thank you." They were making small talk, meaningless chatter, and it suddenly occurred to her that Claude was less at ease than he'd been in London. Then, he had been the aggressor, storming into her life and demanding that she come here because it suited his purposes. Now that she was here, she would be living in his home, with his mother and sister, and young Henri . . . and suddenly the situation was subtly changing. Tania wondered briefly just what his womenfolk had thought of his emotional blackmail in bringing her here. Or if they even knew of his strong-arm tactics!

She glanced at his profile as he sat beside her in his sleek sports car ten minutes later. It was strong, a determined face that she had seen change to a gentleness she wouldn't have suspected, when he spoke of his nephew. She shivered for no reason. James had once told her the mountains sorted out the wheat from the chaff, choosing for their own the men fit to scale them. James had been one of them, until the accident.

Claude was certainly another, if strength of character and powerful physique were trademarks. How long before another accident robbed another woman of her son . . . her lover . . . ? She was still afraid of shadows . . . but when the shadows were of the implacable, forbidding mountains, demanding every respect from mere vulnerable humans, then yes. She was afraid of shadows.

"You're very quiet." Claude's voice made her start. She had turned from him to gaze out at the changing countryside. Vineyards to the south of Bordeaux; a confluence of rivers with lovely old stone bridges; fertile, hot land that gradually gave way to drier, more arid country, and a more mountainous region.

"I'm trying to decide just what I'm doing here," she muttered. "It's the last place I expected to be."

He put his hand on her knee for a brief moment, before giving all his attention to the steeply climbing road.

"You're here because I want you to be. It's what James would have wanted, too."

Tania shivered again, despite the heat. There was a note of inevitability in his voice, and she had the uneasy feeling that James's wishes might be secondary to his. It was Claude who wanted her here. James's feelings were a useful ploy to get her here. Emotional blackmail, she thought again, and it had worked. She didn't want to dwell on it.

"I hadn't expected your home to be so far south," she said instead.

He looked mildly surprised. "Didn't James ever tell you anything about it?"

"He tried. I didn't listen." She didn't care what Claude made of that. "I loved my brother, but I didn't love his obsession with the mountains, and the less I knew about it the better."

"I told you once before that you make it sound almost immoral." He sounded amused, and Tania flushed, because she hadn't meant that at all. Claude knew that very well, she guessed, and he wasn't going to provoke her. She shrugged.

"I don't know this part of France at all. I know Paris and the surrounding area, and once, when James and I were small, we spent a ghastly four days under canvas in the pouring rain on the Brittany coast, while our parents did some research for a marine-life project." She shuddered, remembering.

Claude laughed, stopping her nervous flow of words. Tania was annoyed at knowing that she really did feel nervous. New country, new people, and Claude Girard beside her, who was enough to unnerve any woman. Tania was even more annoyed at herself for being so spineless! She met new people all the time in her job. Often she was the only person able to converse with the strangers who came to look over the engineering plants belonging to the company. She was competent and assured in her work, but in Claude Girard's presence, she was aware of a disturbing lack of self-confidence. She didn't like the feeling one bit.

"Any time you feel the need for bright lights, Biarritz is within driving distance of the château," Claude commented. "My home is fairly isolated, Tania, but I hope you will like it. I want you to feel it is your home too."

When they stopped at a café for a drink just outside Toulouse, the blue haze of towering mountains to the south was very evident. Tania's geography was sketchy, and Claude supplied the information.

"The Pyrenees," he informed her. "They form the border between France and Spain. The château is well situated for marvellous views, and also to give me speedy access for any rescue activities."

"Do you operate from the château?"

"Of course. You will see my operations room." Claude grinned. "It looks something like a military operations room, with the most modern equipment. Any climber in danger on the mountains can get in touch with us or base camp hook-ups, by means of walkie-talkie radios. We don't just wander over the mountains looking for stray hikers, Tania."

"And this is what James was involved in?" She was embarrassed not to have known about it more fully. This stupid block she had had about learning too deeply of the dangers of his life . . .

"I can see you need to be educated a little more, _chérie_," Claude said lightly. "It will be my pleasure to teach you."

The inflexion in his voice told her instinctively that it wasn't only the detail of his work that he wanted to teach her. Perhaps it was only because of what James had mentioned casually about this man – his interest in women, his need to live life to the full, added to his determination to get her here, and the way in which he had succeeded – whatever the reason, Tania was perfectly sure that Claude would find it amusing to add her to his list of conquests. And she was equally sure that he would not succeed.

The daylight was beginning to fade a little, though the air was warm and still by the time Claude pulled the car to a halt on a narrow, hilly road. Tania's heart began to thud a little. There was nothing here . . . She turned to him suspiciously, but he was getting out of the car and coming round to open her door.

"Come," he said softly. "A stranger's first sight of the Château Girard should be from a high ridge, to see the last of the sunlight glinting down on it."

He took her hand in his, and Tania walked beside him as he led her twenty-odd yards farther on, where the road curved to the left.

And then she saw it. She gasped. Far below, in a deep valley, was the most beautiful and magnificent castle she had ever seen. And this – this was Claude's home! She felt dumb with shock, as the grey pointed turrets of the typical French château glinted like liquid pewter in the sun, as Claude had said. James had never told her anything about this! Or if he had, she simply hadn't listened . . .

"We have a family legend, Tania. A stranger's first sight of the château must also be accompanied by a kiss, to ensure a true welcome and good fortune."

He had pulled her into his arms before she could make any trite remark. Before she could protest, she was moulded to his athletic body, her back arching towards him by the pressure of his hands, and her own capitulation. For it was all part of a dream . . . this beautiful French château, and Claude, the undoubted king of all he surveyed . . . She had mumbled something about him being medieval, she could believe it even more now. There was something primitive about the way he was claiming her kiss as his right. It was more than a welcome to a stranger. There was passion and need and a deep sensuality in the way his mouth was possessing hers now, and Tania was as powerless to resist as a leaf in the wind.

Her arms had been rigidly at her sides while she drank in the beauty of the panorama below them. Now, as if they moved of their own accord, they reached upwards to encircle Claude's broad back. She could feel the strength of his muscles beneath her fingers. Everywhere their bodies touched, she was aware of power and strength, and of taut masculinity. She was hardly aware that her fingers dug into his back as a flame of desire more potent than anything she had ever known before seemed to sear her body.

As effective as a total act of love, Claude's charisma seemed to envelop her, telling her of his needs more clearly than mere words. His mouth had demanded all that he wanted of her, gently prising her own apart, until she felt the probing of his tongue against hers, erotic and arousing. With a shock of awareness, Tania knew the most pleasurable sensations she had ever experienced as his blatant assault on her went on, and on . . . her breasts were crushed against him, as if straining to be part of him, wanting him, wanting more . . .

Finally, Claude's mouth tugged softly at her full bottom lip, as if he would have his last sweet fill of her. He still held her in the circle of his arms, his mouth touching hers, as he murmured soft words to her.

"Welcome stranger. I think the good fortune must be mine, to have found you. The Girards have long been known for a fiercely possessive clan, Tania. Girard men never relinquish their women, once they find the one that is their destiny."

The sudden cry of a high-wheeling bird and a fluttering of wings in the foliage of tall trees broke the supercharged moment, to Tania's wild relief. For what seemed like hours, she felt as if she had been held in some kind of spell, bewitched by Claude Girard's dark eyes and compelling presence. And she was half-frightened by the way her senses had reached out to meet him halfway, as if he was her soul-mate, her destiny . . .

His intensity, and the vibrant words he had spoken, were in such odd contrast with the playboy image she had always had of him, that she was totally confused by her feelings. Then, too, so was the caring way he had spoken of young Henri, and the obvious dedication she sensed in his mountain rescue work. She couldn't have got him all wrong all this time, could she? She didn't want to think so. She wanted to keep her feelings on an even keel regarding him, and not to have this heady, swirling delight running through her because Claude Girard had kissed her, and somehow touched her soul in doing so.

"Hadn't we better be moving on?" Her voice was slightly cracked, and she didn't look into his eyes. She didn't want him to read there what she wouldn't yet admit to herself. "Won't your mother be expecting us?"

Claude gave a low laugh, as if he knew exactly what she was thinking. "All right, my little English pigeon. Soon, you'll discover you have wings to fly, like the birds in the trees, and then you and I will soar to the heights together."

She almost fled back to the car, her face burning at his words, his meaning crystal clear. What on earth was the matter with her? Tania asked herself furiously. She was reacting like a schoolgirl instead of a warm, passionate, mature woman, just because Claude had made it obvious that he desired her. It was the most natural thing in the world for a man to feel desire for a woman. It was the very essence of life. Every woman needed to feel desired and loved . . . Tania blinked her eyes angrily. She didn't seek love from Claude Girard. It wasn't love that he offered. The thought was suddenly a piquant one.

"Oh, by the way," Claude said casually, as he steered the car around the narrow bends on the descent to the château. "I wouldn't comment on the family legend to anyone, if I were you, Tania. It's rather a private one— "

"You made it up!" she blazed at him, all the ethereal feelings gone in a moment. "And by a private one, I suppose you mean it's the one the lordly Claude Girard uses whenever he brings a pretty woman to his home! I might have guessed it!"

"Why? Did you have quite such a preconceived bad opinion of me?" he said tightly, annoyed at her violent reaction.

"The worst," she snapped. "And it's quite obvious now that it was the right one."

"It's just as obvious that I was all wrong about you," Claude retorted. "I couldn't really believe that anyone as lovely as you could be such a shrew! Do all your men-friends get treated to this display every time they kiss you? Or is it the sort of thing an Englishman expects? Your brother was obviously the exception to the rule. He was refreshingly normal!"

She clamped her lips shut, refusing to be baited by his insults, or the reference to James. He wasn't getting around her that way. He was despicable, just as she had always guessed he would be. The sooner she could get to work on the book that he needed her for and back to England, the better. She needed the calm stability of David's easy companionship. She didn't need the volatile, explosive passion of Claude Girard!

He said no more as they drove the last part of the journey to his home, but as he jerked the car to a stop, he turned to her, his voice expressionless.

"If we can at least manage to be civil to each other, it will be more comfortable for us all, Tania," he said.

"As long as we remember this is a business arrangement, I see no problem," she said distantly.

He muttered an expletive in French beneath his breath, and Tania smiled faintly, understanding perfectly. What was it he really wanted of her? she thought in bewilderment. He hadn't really brought her all this way on some mad seductive whim, had he? It was hardly likely. Why her, when he could have the pick of France's high-society women if he chose? It was beginning to dawn on her just how wealthy the Girard family must be. And as the only son, Claude would be a catch for any woman. Why bother with a reluctant Englishwoman he referred to as a shrew! Tania smarted, recalling the word. It was completely unjustified, but let him think it. What did she care?

A manservant Claude addressed as Alphonse appeared from the château to take the baggage. It was another world. Inside the château it was cool and seemingly vast. Marble floors and costly paintings added to the unreality of the place for Tania. It was more like a museum . . . And then the silver-haired lady she had seen in Claude's snapshots came out to greet them, and at once the ambience of the place changed. There was real warmth and affection in Madame Girard's face as she kissed her son and then turned to Tania, hands outstretched. There was a hint of a tear in her dark eyes, so like Claude's.

"My dear Tania, at last we make our acquaintance," she spoke in English as good as Claude's. "Our dear James spoke of you so often, I feel as if I know you already. You are so exactly as he painted you, though even prettier. Such beautiful hair, and that enviable English complexion! Come and meet Monique. She, too, is longing to see if you live up to James's ideal!"

Tania was acutely embarrassed as Madame went on in this fashion. She had known nothing of this family until a week ago, and yet it seemed that they knew a great deal about her! She was ashamed at shutting James out of her life because of her fear for him, and in so doing, had been quite unaware of his second family, which, it was becoming more and more obvious, was how the Girards looked on themselves. Thinking back, she knew how often James had tried to draw her into his life . . . even Claude would have prepared her, had she not cut him short at every opportunity. She only had herself to blame if she sat and squirmed now.

She needn't have worried too much. Claude's family were far too well bred to allow any guest to feel embarrassment. Tania liked Claude's sister at once. Monique was very like him, though a few years older. She was handsome, rather than pretty. Her hands were ringless, except for a large, old-fashioned diamond cluster, maybe the only memento of her dead husband, Tania surmised.

"Would you like some food, Tania?" Monique asked,

once they had been introduced. "We have eaten but it would only take a moment— "

"No thank you," Tania said quickly. "Just coffee, if you don't mind. I'm feeling quite tired, in fact."

"Then Claude will show you to your room whenever you're ready,' Madame smiled. "And tomorrow we will talk at our leisure, my dear."

She rang a bell in the wall, and spoke into a tube. It could have come straight out of a film set, Tania thought. In a very short time, coffee was brought by a maid, and she began to realise just how tired she was. It wasn't so much the travelling as the tension of coming here, and being with Claude again. She was willing to admit that much. Love him or hate him, she found it impossible to be indifferent to him. When she had finished her coffee, he asked her if she was ready. She said goodnight to the women, feeling a little strange to be leaving the room with Claude. It was ridiculous, and she knew it, but she couldn't change the way she felt.

He led her through endless corridors and stairs, and Tania thought she would never find her way down again. Finally they reached a long corridor with a door at the far end.

"My quarters are through there," he reminded her of the oddly phrased words, "I wanted you near to me, to make it easier for working arrangements, so your room is at the end of this corridor."

He spoke blandly, but Tania's heart thumped all the same. Easier for working arrangements – or for some other arrangement?

"I'll show you the lay-out tomorrow," Claude went on, unaware that her pulse was racing at the implications spinning round in her head. Or maybe he was perfectly aware . . .

"Claude – is that you? I wanted to wait up, but Maman wouldn't let me."

The words were spoken in French, but quite understandable to Tania. It was a childish voice, and Claude stopped, with a quick word of apology as he retraced his steps along the corridor from where they had come. Tania hesitated, not sure which door she should open, finally deciding to follow slowly. It wasn't hard to track down the whoops of delight coming from Henri's room as he greeted his adored uncle, and Tania heard Claude's quick explanation that the present he'd brought the boy from Bordeaux must wait until morning, or Henri's mother would have his hide.

Through the open doorway of Henri's room, Tania saw the small wheelchair by the bedside. Apart from that, and the fact that all the furniture was carefully placed to give the wheelchair and its occupant a clear passage through the room, there was nothing to say that the child was handicapped. Certainly there was nothing to distinguish Henri from any other child at that moment as he flung his arms around Claude's neck and hugged him, nor the obvious affection that existed between the two as Claude gathered the small boy tenderly in his arms and then laid it gently back against the pillows.

Tania felt an emotional lump in her throat at the sight of them both. Here was love, she thought tremblingly. If she had ever thought Claude Girard incapable of giving or receiving it, such suspicions were extinguished in a single moment. In their place was a very different emotion, one that she couldn't readily analyse. Pity for the small boy, locked within his own frail body by a tragic accident? A feeling of wanting to tip-toe away, not wanting to witness these very private moments between two people with such a great empathy for one another? A grudging warmth towards Claude, for bringing such radiance to a child's face? A sudden sharp tingle of something like envy, that it wasn't she who was being held so tenderly in Claude's arms . . . ?

It was all these, and more, crystallised into one gigantic surge of emotion towards Claude Girard. It was as if the tightly locked bitterness she'd held against him for so long, was slowly disintegrating. In a crazy, inexplicable way, it was as painfully pleasurable as the feeling of being reborn.

Chapter 4

She slept surprisingly well. Despite the strange surroundings and the odd silence after the noise of London's traffic around her flat, Tania found the heat of the south had an almost drugging effect on her, like jet-lag. When she commented on it to Madame Girard next day, she was assured it would soon pass.

"I hope so, otherwise I shall fall asleep as soon as Claude and I start work." She was conscious of her heart giving a little flip as she spoke his name. "Where is he, by the way?"

The two of them were taking breakfast. To Tania's relief, a maid had been hovering near her room when she came out, to direct her through the maze of the château's corridors.

"He takes Henri through his exercises each morning," Madame told her quietly. "You'll have heard about the child, I'm sure, Tania?"

"Oh yes." Guiltily, Tania wondered if Madame assumed that James would have told her, and she was thankful now that Claude had told her about his family. Madame Girard gave a small sigh.

"Claude is so devoted to the boy. It's a tragedy – but it does not do to dwell on it. Claude says we must think positively, and hope that an operation will prove possible.

Meanwhile, he does everything to make the boy's life as comfortable as he can. No woman could wish for a better son.''

"If you go on in that way, Tania will have to reverse her bad opinions of me, Mother.'' Claude's mocking voice came from the doorway of the dining-room. He pushed Henri's wheelchair into the room, and the boy looked shyly at the stranger. From his pallor, Tania wondered just how painful the exercises were that the child had to do. She felt a great wave of compassion for him, and her embarrassment at Claude's words was covered quickly by Madame Girard's indulgent laugh. It was obvious from the affection between them that she didn't really believe anyone could have a bad opinion of her son! Tania was conscious of a sudden feeling of loss. Absurdly sharp, it was the recognition of this close-knit, loving family, which was so vastly different from her own.

The love of her parents had never been the driving force in her life – or James's. They had cared for the children as patiently as they would any small animal in their care that needed nurturing and careful attention. But with their wider interests, the Paget parents had never given their children that one vital essential – their time. Whatever else Henri lacked, he didn't lack love, or company.

He spoke in rapid French to Claude. Tania blushed as Claude laughed, his eyes dancing at her, as he replied equally quickly to Henri in the same language.

"Tania understands all that you say, *mon petit*! She will tell you about England if you ask her, I am sure. And yes, I agree. She is a very pretty lady."

"When we wish to converse privately, we speak in English," Madame said quietly to Tania. "Henri does

62

not learn the language yet, though he wishes to, and has picked up a few words."

"Perhaps I can teach him some while I'm here," Tania heard herself say. Now why had she done that! It just seemed to be one small thing she could offer to the handicapped child, and she heard Claude repeat her words to Henri, whose face smiled in delight at this unexpected bonus. Unexpected to Henri . . . yet Tania had the suspicious thought that Claude had intended her to suggest this all along. She couldn't explain the feeling. There was just something in the little quirk of his mouth that said he was pleased she was integrating herself into his home as smoothly as he had planned.

She mentally shook herself. She was imagining things. Why should Claude want her here any longer than was necessary to help him on his book? From the way she'd shown her dislike of him, he'd be more likely to make their acquaintance as short as possible! She stopped pondering, and spoke to Henri instead, in perfect French.

"I'm very happy to meet you, Henri. I'll make a bargain with you. I'll tell you about England, and you tell me about France. I've never been in a château before."

"Don't they have them in England?" Henri's curiosity overcame his shyness, and Tania laughed.

"We call them castles, *chéri*. We have plenty of those, but the Queen lives in a palace."

"Will you tell me about the Queen and her palace?" Henri said eagerly.

"Later, Henri," his grandmother stepped in with a smile, as the child's eagerness grew. "First you must have your rest, and then your lessons with the tutor."

Henri pulled a face, and said quickly that he'd rather

63

be taught by the pretty English lady than Monsieur de Lyons.

"I can't say that I blame him," Claude grinned, when his mother had taken Henri out of the room. His eyes looked approvingly at the pale blue skirt and thin shirt Tania wore. She wasn't too sure how one dressed in a château, but decided that it was best to wear her normal mode of dress rather than try to impress anybody. Simple styles suited her far better than any fancy attempts at sophistication and gave her the cool English look that was envied by many Continental women. There was admiration in Claude's eyes at that moment.

"The tutor comes here, does he?" Tania ignored the compliment to herself, and Claude nodded.

"He teaches him geography and French history, and the rudiments of schooling. He's a bright little boy, as you have seen. He'll respond quickly to your English lessons— "

"I haven't said I'll give him lessons— " Somehow it was getting away from her. She had the feeling that whatever Claude Girard wanted, Claude Girard got.

"I'm sure you will. Who could refuse Henri?"

It wasn't Henri he expected her not to refuse. It was as clear as crystal. She made one more objection.

"What of his tutor? He won't take kindly to an English woman taking over some of his duties!"

"He's paid to do as he's asked," Claude said calmly. "The Girards are a generous family. We expect the best and we get it. I want you, Tania. If it pleases you to have it all arranged on a business level, then you too will be paid for teaching Henri English."

It was ludicrous. A week ago, she had been perfectly happy working in London. Now this man had bought her

64

time away from the company and was offering her more payment in teaching his handicapped nephew, as well as letting her share his lovely home while she gave him background information on her brother for his book. She rebelled at the smooth assumption that he could buy anything he wanted. She wasn't being bought.

"I don't want payment, thank you. It will be my pleasure to give Henri some English lessons while I am here. After that, I've no doubt you can find him an English teacher if Monsieur de Lyons isn't competent enough."

Her frigid tone did nothing to irritate Claude. Instead as he came across the room to her, his large frame suddenly filling the space between them, she saw that he was laughing at her.

"My prim little Tania," he said softly, as he reached her. "You have the Englishwoman's knack of creating an untouchable shell around yourself, quicker than blinking. It is even more intriguing when everything else about you gives the impression of the very opposite. All my instincts tell me that beneath that icy exterior beats a very warm and loving heart. It only waits for the right man to awaken you."

Tania hoped that he couldn't see how her heart was beating very fast right at that minute. Claude's voice was very seductive when it was lowered, and it unnerved her to have this instant character-analysis made of her. She felt exposed to him, and she didn't altogether like the feeling. All those years when she and James had been kept apart from each other, and from their parents, she had developed a kind of brittle self-defence. She had never let herself care too much for anyone, keeping male admirers at arm's length except on a platonic level. She was afraid to let herself fall in love . . . and until she had met Claude

Girard, she had never fully admitted it to herself before. She hated him for making her face herself properly, and for his assured assessment of her. He must have known many women, Tania thought bitterly.

Known them and loved them. And to her mind, such men degraded the very name of love. The woman in her rebelled at mere sexual gratification. Without deep, passionate love, it was meaningless. Tania swallowed, as the words burned into her mind. Why should she care if Claude Girard had loved and seduced a thousand woman! It was nothing to her, nothing at all.

"I would much rather we kept our minds on business," she said abruptly. She caught her breath as Claude put his hands on her shoulders. His fingers moved very gently, as if to remind her by his caressing movements that by his very maleness he could bend her to his will whenever he chose. She fought not to react, holding her whole body in check, and only succeeding in telling him by her tenseness that she was far from being unaware of him. He looked searchingly into her amber eyes, as if seeking the answer to a question not yet spoken.

"Business is such a cold word between you and me, *chérie*," he said finally. "Between a man and a woman is all the glory of the universe, and my cold little Tania speaks only of business! No Frenchwoman would be so heartless!"

She felt her cheeks burn. Was he trying to tell her any other woman would have fallen into his bed by now? Tania tried to think logically, though it was difficult to do so when those seductive fingers continued to make their tantalising little explorations of her shoulders and the hollows of her neck. Why didn't she break away? It was as if she was held in a kind of trance. He'd never asked her to go to bed with him, she reminded herself, almost hysterically, but the only way he hadn't asked her was with words. Everything else – his eyes, his voice, his entire charismatic animal appeal, from the smouldering, sensual looks, to the broad chest with its covering of hair visible in the open neck of his checked shirt, to the tautly muscled thighs in his light slacks – everything about him told her he wanted to make love to her. Tania ran the tip of her tongue around her dry lips.

She had only met him a week ago. She had seen him on a few occasions, though in reality it seemed as if she had known him far longer. Through James . . . For all that she had kept Claude's image strictly out of her consciousness whenever her brother spoke of him or wrote of him or sent newspaper cuttings of him, Tania knew that the knowledge of this man had somehow seeped into her subconsciousness the whole time.

If a stranger asked her questions about him, from some-where in that wealth of knowledge she had assimilated without knowing it, she could have answered him. It was an uncanny feeling to know it.

"I'm not a Frenchwoman," she snapped, more dis-turbed than she would have guessed at the unwanted affinity between them. "And unless you got me here under false pretences, I suggest you show me your study or wherever it is you work, and let's get some work done."

Claude pretended to back off. "All right! James was right about you, Tania. You have a bite to you! Very well. We'll work until lunchtime. After that, Henri and I always swim. The human body is remarkably buoyant in water, even when the muscles are too weak to support it in air. I'm sure you'll be glad to join us. The afternoon heat is sometimes intense."

To her relief he let her go. His words evoked a mixture of annoyance and curiosity.

"Do you have a swimming-pool at the château?"

"Of course." Claude spoke as if everyone did. "We also have a small indoor one for use during the winter. It is important for Henri to have the exercise."

Obviously, nothing was too good for the child. Tania felt a grudging admiration for Claude for making everything as easy and comfortable as he could for his nephew. She realised she hadn't seen Monique that morning, and enquired after her.

"Monique owns an exclusive little boutique in Toulouse. She has no need to go there each day, except for her own self-preservation. She has been through a lot in recent years. It's good for her and Henri to spend some time apart too. They tend to rely too heavily on one another, and each must learn to be self-reliant. Do you understand me?"

"Yes, I do." It was a completely different kind of self-reliance from her own parents' dismissal of her and James. Monique could smother Henri by her lavish love, and the child needed to feel capable of doing things for himself. She hadn't needed to be here very long to realise they were a typically emotional French family.

They left the dining-room just as Madame Girard came back to look for Tania.

"Claude isn't going to start work with you already, is he? I thought you'd like to look around the château, my dear."

"Tania wishes to work, Mother," he told her. "I'll show her around later. And don't feel obliged to stay at home from your charity meeting this afternoon. Tania will join Henri and me in the pool."

Tania didn't miss the faint relief in Madame's eyes. She

68

realised that it may sound as if Claude was taking over, but she had to remember too, that his family had their own lives to lead, and she wasn't there as a normal guest, after all. She couldn't expect everything to revolve around her. She confirmed Claude's words quickly, slightly chagrined at doing so, but not really having any other choice.

The sound of a car on the gravel drive meant the arrival of Monsieur de Lyons, Madame told Tania. She hurried away to greet him and to tell him that Henri was ready for him. Tania got a glimpse of a dour-faced, middle-aged man as he approached the château from his car.

"Shall we go?" Claude said in the small silence. "My quarters await you, *ma belle* Tania."

The slight mocking note was back in his voice again. Ignoring it, she followed him through the lower corridors to a heavy oak door. On the other side of it was Claude's bachelor establishment, into which no-one went without invitation or permission. One day the entire château would be his, but in his quarters, he was already king. He gave her a brief look round before entering the study, and one room in particular drew her undoubted respect.

It wasn't a room she could like. On every wall were maps and charts of the mountains, those in the immediate vicinity, and those farther afield. There were red areas marked in, which Claude explained were the danger areas, and every known facet of them was marked meticulously. The room was businesslike, the centre of the mountain rescue operation headquarters. There were two desks, with phones and recording equipment, and Tania had the feeling that Claude would be out of here in seconds if a rescue was needed. As if to confirm the thought, he pointed to a contraption on one of the desks.

"We're trying out a new system of communication with

walkie-talkies for climbers. As long as they remember to switch on, we can record their movements and warn them of any changing weather conditions and so on, especially any soft snow traps or impending blizzards.''

It was hard to think of such things right then, with the sun blazing down from a brilliant blue sky. She didn't want to think of them. It reminded her too much of James.

"My assistant, Marc, will be here soon," Claude said. "But if you've seen enough, we'll go into the study. My notes are all pretty chaotic, I warn you. I'm not a writer, as I said. I prefer doing the climbs than writing about them, but James always did have a hankering to see our work put down in print for posterity.''

Tania had certainly seen enough of the rescue operations room. Marc must be the new assistant. James had been Claude's partner and the two of them had been the team here . . . The whole thing was becoming more of an emotional strain than she had imagined. She thought she had got used to her brother's death. Six months had dulled the pain a little, and dulled also the useless regrets that theirs had never been a really close relationship. Now, suddenly, all the sorrow was back with her again, stabbing at her with little emotional pin-pricks, each time she thought of James here in these rooms. Sharing the love of the mountains, the dangers and the exhilarations Tania simply couldn't understand, this environment somehow brought him very near. She hadn't felt so close to him since his death.

Claude showed her into his study. His desk was a jumble of files and papers massed around a typewriter. One file had fallen to the floor, and Tania automatically bent to pick it up. Several glossy photos of James fell out. Laughing, full of the youthful vitality she remembered, looking into her eyes with all his enthusiasm for living, confident, in a way Tania had never been confident. Because James had found what he wanted out of life, and she had not – not yet.

As she looked at the photos, they suddenly blurred in front of her, and her hands trembled. Then her whole body was gripped in a gigantic bout of shaking. She couldn't seem to stop. It seemed an eternity that she stood there, feeling as if the earth was shifting beneath her feet, crumbling into nothingness. She felt as James must have felt plunging from the mountain, with nothing, nothing . . .

From the sudden coldness she felt, Tania was suddenly warmed by Claude's arms. Hardly knowing that she did so, she was rocked against the hardness of his body, while the releasing tears she had been unable to shed for so long burst from her like a dam unleashed. She sobbed against him, uncaring that she proved herself vulnerable at last. Not even thinking of him in any way but a pair of strong arms to support her and hold her when she most needed support.

And Claude, forgetting everything but that she turned to him, and clung to him, murmured soft, comforting words in her ears. Forgetting that she understood his language as if it was her native tongue, he murmured words of love to her, over and over, telling her that she need be afraid of nothing ever again. That she was here, where she belonged, where she had always belonged . . .

The words swam in and out of Tania's senses, little more than a sweet warm panacea to her pain. His voice was a soothing narcotic, no more, and for the moment she never heeded or looked for any meaning behind it.

Finally, the paroxysm was over, and Tania leaned weakly against Claude. Trembling with embarrassment now, she raised her swollen eyes to his face. He was against the light, and she couldn't really see the expression in his own eyes. She swallowed thickly.

"Thank you – for being here just then," she whispered. "I'm – I'm sorry if I – I embarrassed you."

His answer was a short sharp oath, and then he gathered her in his arms again.

"Don't ever apologise for being a woman," he said roughly. "As for my being here – I'll always be here, whenever you need me. I thought I'd made that plain to you, *chérie*."

Before she could decide whether he was playing the sincere friend or the would-be seducer, his mouth was crushing hers in a kiss that was more like an assault on her senses than an embrace. A hard, demanding kiss, from a man to a woman, leaving her in no doubt that he wanted her. Every taut muscle in his body told her so. His hands moved up and down her back, finding the curve of her waist, and the roundness of her hips, pressing her to him in a wordless enfolding of her body to his.

Tania felt weightless, floating. Heat suffused every part of her. She felt safe, cherished . . . how could she feel safe, in the arms of this man who courted danger as if it held all the fascination of a beautiful woman? Yet perhaps safe wasn't quite the word she would use to describe her feelings. There was an excitement leaping inside her, as if the spot wherever his skin touched hers was suddenly scalding, not painfully, but more pleasurably than anything Tania had known before . . .

She wrenched herself out of his arms. Claude Girard stood for danger, and never had she been more conscious of that danger than right now. He was dangerous to her. He said he would be here whenever she needed him, but she was all too aware of Claude's needs.

"Can we work – *please*?" she said, in a strangled voice. "I'll try and detach myself from getting too personally involved if I can. At least, I'll promise not to cry all over you again."

"I wasn't objecting to the experience." He sounded angry, displeased. Perhaps he'd thought she was ready to forget work, and that being with him had superceded all else.

Her chin lifted. "I rarely cry," she stated. Into her mind came the unbidden, half-forgotten memory of her mother telling her in that remote way of hers that being sent away to school was for the best. That it would form her character. That she mustn't cry, because tears were a sign of weakness. She gave a perceptible laugh.

"Laying ghosts?" Claude said gently. So typically English a phrase, said with that intriguing accent, stilled the sharp retort on her lips, and she nodded woodenly. As if sensing that she had come a long way in a very short time, Claude led her to a chair and sat her down in it. It was quite a relief, because Tania suddenly realised her legs began to feel as if they wouldn't hold her up much longer. He became brisk, perched on the edge of the desk and giving her time to control her tumbling thoughts as he outlined his proposals for the book.

Most of it, Tania would be unable to help him with. But all the background work, the intimate part of James's early life, in which she played so much a part, she certainly could. A spark of interest began to revitalise her after the emotional outburst that had left her so drained and empty.

A feeling that maybe Claude was right after all. This was for James. It was what he would have wanted. And Tania was the only one who could ensure that anyone reading the book would have the true picture of his childhood. A sliver of warmth returned to her cold limbs. It was directed towards Claude. He had made this possible. Maybe she owed him something after all. Maybe in giving him an account of her recollections of James, she would in some way exorcise the painful ghosts of the past and face the future with more confidence.

From somewhere in the château a bell sounded. Tania flexed her back muscles from the cuttings she and Claude had been poring over, and she glanced at her watch. Her mouth dropped open as she realised the time.

"That's Alphonse's idea, ringing the bell for lunch," Claude told her with a smile. "We tend to scatter about the place, and the bell can be heard just about everywhere. We've done enough for one day, anyway."

"We've hardly rippled the surface," Tania said ruefully.

He smiled at her. "That's all right. I have six months of your time, remember? If we get the book finished in too much of a hurry, you'll want to go back to England, and I've no intention of letting you escape that easily!"

His smile was like that of the tiger, lazy in its certainty that it could toy as much as it wanted to with its prey.

"And I've no intention of being held here for six months," she said breathlessly. She noted that she often felt breathless when he gave her one of his intense looks, as if he was exerting some intangible power over her. She would never succumb to it.

"You speak as if the château is a prison," he said, amused, dismissing her words as if they were of no importance. "If you think that, Tania, I hope you will admit that it's the most beautiful, luxurious prison you ever saw!"

"I won't deny that," she retorted. "And I hope you will admit that I came here voluntarily, and that I'm free to leave whenever I wish!"

Her eyes challenged his. He saw the fire in their amber depths. His own were veiled, the lids heavy, half-closed, as the tiger's smile played around his mouth.

"But of course," he said simply. "Whenever you wish."

Tania shivered, as if the silken threads that held them in a shared venture were subtly spinning closer together, enmeshing them in a tapestry from which there was no escaping. It wasn't the place. It was the man.

He opened the long french doors of the study to allow them a walk back around the walls of the château to the dining-room. It was so easy for Tania to lose all sense of direction, but she realised that for all its age, the château was installed with efficient air-conditioning. As soon as they stepped outside, the motionless, mid-day air hit them like a blast of furnace heat. Tania's fair skin prickled, and after the concentration of the morning, the thought of an afternoon swim in cool, refreshing water, was a very enticing one.

Monique wasn't there at lunchtime. Madame told Tania that her daughter needed the outside stimulus to recover from her mental trauma after the child's accident, and then her husband's death. These people had known tragedy too, Tania thought. And the fact that Madame talked to her quite freely about it didn't seem odd at all. They didn't treat her as a stranger, because to them she wasn't a stranger. James had spoken of her too often for that.

Briefly ashamed at the way she had blocked out any

reference to Claude or his family from her own letters to her brother, Tania gave James credit for having a better nature than she did! Or at least a more extrovert one, and it was obvious that in speaking of his sister, James had never said anything bad about her. He had never let them know how much she disapproved of his mountaineering or his friends who lived as reckless a life as he did. Reckless, to Tania's mind . . .

"Can I sit by Tania for lunch?" Henri said, when Claude appeared behind his wheelchair a few minutes later.

"You've made another conquest," Claude smiled at her, and she concentrated on moving the wheelchair close to the table, rather than look into Claude's eyes. Another conquest? Did he mean he was the first? Tania's mouth twisted a little. She thought Claude did all the conquering . . . or tried to.

"I just talked to Maman on the telephone," Henri gabbled excitedly in his quick French accent. "She says Denis is coming to stay for the weekend. We will take a picnic to the sea."

"It sounds lovely," Tania murmured, not knowing who Denis might be. Claude supplied the answer in English.

"Denis is Monique's fiancé. She has known him for years, and steadfastly refused to become engaged to him, meaning to devote her life to Henri, until we persuaded her how foolish that was. A child can only benefit by having a good stepfather, and Denis is the best. Though when the wedding will be is another matter. Monique is very stubborn when she chooses." His mouth curved into a smile. "It runs in the family, Tania. We all go after what we want with determination."

"I can't understand you!" Henri's small voice said plaintively. "Is it about me and Maman?"

76

Claude laughed, ruffling his hair. "Do you think we have nothing else to talk about, you vain little peacock?"

"You spoke my name, and Maman's," Henri pouted.

"So I did," Claude told him. "But you will have to wait until you learn English to find out just what I said."

"Grandmère " The child swivelled in the wheelchair in protest, and she laughed gently, telling the boy that his uncle was only teasing him, and it was merely to tell Mademoiselle Tania a little about their life here.

"I must learn English as soon as possible then," Henri said, with Girard determination. "Then I will understand everything."

"Serves you right for suggesting it," Tania murmured to Claude beneath her breath as the mutinous little look came into Henri's eyes. Mention that Monique had a fiancé had surprised her somewhat, though there was no reason why it should. Though if she did marry again, and she and her Denis set up home away from the château, she was certain that Henri would be very much missed. That he was doted on was very obvious, and understandably so in the circumstances. Maybe the child played on it now and then, but to Tania's eyes he seemed pretty well adjusted, considering his limitations.

Madame Girard would miss him very much. Unless, of course, Claude married and provided the Girard family with children. It was inevitable that Madame must hope for that. It was the way of all wealthy families with huge estates . . . Tania bit into her crusty bread roll, realising that her heart was beating more quickly at the thought of Claude having a wife and children.

She vaguely remembered James telling her jocularly once that he didn't think Claude was the marrying type.

77

He was a target for the ladies, and he'd had more than one serious love in his life, but as for marrying . . .

"We'll have an hour's rest after lunch, Tania, and then go to the pool. You'll join us, won't you? It will be too hot for doing anything else this afternoon, though if you wish, I'll show you the rest of the château before we swim."

Claude's voice seemed to come to her out of a mist, and she had to concentrate hard on what he was saying. For crazy moments, she had been transported away from the elegant dining-room, imagining herself moving slowly towards him in a drift of white tulle and lace. The scent of orange-blossom was heady in her nostrils, and there was only love in Claude's sardonic dark eyes as he turned to receive her. Only love . . .

Chapter 5

The tour of the château after lunch confirmed Tania's thoughts that her own bedroom with its lovely chintz coverings and deep soft carpet, was only a door away from Claude's. Or to be strictly accurate, several doors. Between them was the end of the corridor, through which Claude had his bachelor quarters. But the first room on the other side of that separating door was Claude's bedroom. Their walls were adjoining.

It was purely coincidental, Tania told herself. It shouldn't matter to her where he slept. And her room was obviously a guest room. The suspicion crept into her mind. How many other young women had spent their nights in the chintz room . . . or not?

"You seem preoccupied, *chérie*," Claude remarked, when she followed him down his own stairs to the lower rooms and out into the rear part of the château's magnificent grounds. "Isn't it the way James told you?"

Tania flushed. Surely Claude must know of her aversion to the mountains, and surely James must have relayed some of her antagonism to him over the years! He was certainly aware that she had refused to open the sports hall at James's old college if Claude Girard attended. He was deliberately mocking her.

"I'm dazzled by it all," she said airily. "It's not every day

79

a working girl finds herself in such princely surroundings. If I was a fortune-hunter, I wouldn't need to look any farther than this!''

It was out of character for her to talk that way, and she only did it to annoy him as he annoyed her. She had hardly expected to see a hot blazing anger in his eyes, nor to feel the cruel grip of his hand on her wrist as he stood still and forced Tania to do the same.

"I don't care to hear you say such things," he snapped. "You degrade yourself by pretending to be something you are not."

"Oh?" Tania was mortified by his aggression, and the knowledge that what he said was true. "What am I, then? Are you so clever that you've done an instant analysis on my character? You don't know anything about me."

Even as she spoke, she knew it wasn't true. He knew too much. But what he knew was second-hand, from her brother. And James had always had a somewhat idealised picture of her. Despite their differences in temperament, he was enormously fond and proud of her, and he would have built her up to something like a goddess on the lonely sojourns on the mountains with Claude. She knew it instinctively.

"I know you in my heart." Claude's words were romantic, but there was nothing romantic in his voice. He was still angry, almost bitter. "You are the woman I have invited into my home, and you are not a fortune-hunter, so don't play with me, Tania. I have no time for such immature games."

"I'm sorry!" She was not. She was affronted at hearing him speak to her like that. As if she was a child! For all his command of the English language and customs, at that moment Claude was very much the dark European, with all the Continental male's superiority over his woman. *His* woman! The brief euphoric moments when Tania had imagined herself as this man's bride were dissipating so fast she knew she'd been absolutely right in disregarding them as nonsense. Any woman who would marry Claude Girard must be a masochist . . .

"No, I'm sorry," he said shortly. "We always seem to be striking a sour note, and it's the last thing I want between us."

"You hope for too much then." His grip on her wrist had slackened, and Tania rubbed at it without thinking, conscious of a slight reddening of her skin where he had held her so fiercely. Claude noticed it, and pulled a face.

"Your skin marks easily," he observed as if she hadn't spoken. "I have some excellent lotion to rub into it while you sunbathe. Don't risk sunburn, Tania, and don't underestimate the strength of the sun here."

"I won't," she answered tartly. "I've already seen that it imparts an atmosphere of prickly heat."

Claude began to laugh. "You must forgive me, but that's one English phrase I don't know," he said, her sarcasm lost on him. "But come and see the pool, and then we'll go in and find Henri. He'll be impatient to be out of doors. He calls his swim the best part of the day."

Tania couldn't argue with that, nor begrudge the child a minute of his pleasure. Claude walked swiftly, covering the ground with his long strides, and she had a job to keep up with him. Then, behind a tall screen of trees, she saw the virginal blue smoothness of the pool, marked out in depths, its surface just asking to be penetrated. The faint tang of chlorine tantalised her nostrils, and it would take an army to keep her away from its inviting coolness, Tania thought fervently.

Claude watched her reaction, smiling faintly.

"Your face betrays your feelings, Tania. At least, it does to me."

"Really?" She tried to slip the cool mask of indifference over her features. "I'll need to take more care in future, then. I'm not sure that I like people knowing when I'm thinking bad thoughts about them!"

"Are they always bad thoughts about me?" He was still amused, refusing to bite.

"Usually— "

"But not always." He laughed more loudly, a note of triumph in the sound. "You can't have it both ways, *ma chérie*. Surely you have some tender thoughts in that hard heart of yours for me?"

"I don't have a hard heart— "

"Ah no. I remember now." At his reflective look, Tania remembered the moment in her flat when she had pressed her hand to her breast in a passionate movement, and through the thin silk Chinese robe Claude had been all too aware of her softness. She turned away from the pool.

"I shall go and change. Hadn't you better fetch Henri? He'll be getting impatient." She spoke with an efficient tone, not letting him know that she remembered any such thing as the moment in her flat. "You said so yourself five minutes ago."

He led her back to the side door of the château.

"Will you be able to find your way back out here? If not, just tap on my bedroom door."

"I'm perfectly capable of finding my own way, thank you," she said quickly, wishing he would take that knowing smile off his face. Why should he think she wanted to go into his bedroom, for any reason whatsoever? She kept her head held high as she went back inside the coolness of the château, away from the oppressive heat that was already making her feel tacky, and want to lift the heavy weight of her hair from her neck. If she ever had second thoughts about taking a swim with Claude, she dismissed them just as quickly. She was quite capable of being in control of herself, however charismatic a man he was. Besides, Henri would be with them. This was Henri's hour, and no time for a clash of personalities between herself and Claude.

In her room, Tania stripped off her garments with a sigh of relief and sought out her bikini and a large towel. She had a lacy coverall to wear over the bikini until she was at the pool, and she put it on quickly, eyeing herself dubiously in the mirror before she did so. The bikini was white and very brief. On a beach in Majorca where half the girls went topless, she had felt almost overdressed in it. Here, in a private pool, with only young Henri and the darkly passionate eyes of Claude Girard to see her, Tania felt conscious of every dip and curve of her body. Knowing that Claude would be aware of them too, because he wasn't the kind of man to ignore a pretty woman.

Tania shrugged. She wanted a swim, and to lie out in that glorious sun. And surely Claude would be preoccupied with Henri for most of the time. This was no time to act like a mouse. She gathered up her towel, slid her feet into some beach mules, and made her way out of the château. Claude hadn't left his room. She knew that, by the small sounds that emanated through the wall between them, of drawers opening and closing, and the occasional humming of a favourite tune. She was glad she would be there first, not to have those sensual eyes watching her approach the pool and slip out of her coverall.

She didn't need his suntan lotion either. She had her own. Tania rubbed it quickly over all her exposed areas of skin and lay back on a lounger to soak up a little sun before she went into the pool. It was sheer bliss to feel the heat relaxing her, slackening all the tense muscles and sending her into an almost mesmeric state . . .

"Don't you have a hat to wear?" Claude's voice said beside her. "You'll regret it if you don't shade your face a little."

Tania's eyes flew open, and then she gasped. He lounged against the steel rail of the steps leading into the pool, as if he posed for some male swimwear magazine.

Tanned to a bronze magnificence, his physique could only be described as stunning. His shoulders were wide, the strength of his muscles apparent with the smallest movement he made. The strong line of his throat and the broad expanse of his chest were covered in rough, dark hair almost down to his navel. He wore black swim briefs, the narrow hips curving outwards and then down to the long, elegantly shaped legs. All the strength he needed to tame the mountains was evident, displayed to perfection for her perusal. Tania realised that she was staring, and knew that her face was tinged with colour, not merely from the sun, but from her own racing pulse. No woman could be unaffected by Claude Girard . . . She moved her tongue around her dry lips.

"Where is Henri?" Her voice sounded thin, as she fought to think ordinary thoughts, instead of the strangely erotic fantasies that were spinning around in her head. She didn't want them there. She didn't ask for them to exist, any more than she had asked to be here, in this French paradise, with Claude Girard's superbly proportioned body paraded in front of her. Tania felt a stab of anger. He did this deliberately of course. Maybe the child wasn't coming here after all. Maybe it had all been a ruse. She would put nothing past Claude.

"Alphonse is bringing him," Claude said calmly, as she sat up, realising that his scrutiny of her had been as intense as hers of him. The two brief scraps of material she wore seemed to be non-existent. She would swear he had the power to see right through them. Uneasily, she remembered that she hadn't worn this bikini in the water before. If it turned out to be transparently thin when it got wet, she would be even more embarrassed than she was now. But she had to risk it. She would prefer to be beneath that enticing blue water than remain here with his hot eyes caressing her in a way more potent than the most physical embrace.

She rose from the lounger in one easy movement, and Claude's eyes flickered over her, in one quick appraisal, and then more slowly, taking his time, wanting and taking his fill of her. The few steps to the edge of the pool seemed to be an endless distance beneath that penetrating gaze. Her hand reached out to take hold of the steel rail, and at the same moment, Claude's fingers trailed lightly up and down her bare arm. As he reached her hand, he turned it over swiftly, turning it palm upwards, and before she could stop him, he had kissed it lightly, and enclosed the point of contact by holding her small hand inside his.

"One small victory, Tania," he said softly. "One kiss that is trapped for ever."

"How can it be? As soon as I open my hand it will be gone." She was as crazy as he, discussing a kiss as if it lived and breathed. To her surprise he let his hand go slack, and she opened her palm at once. "There, you see?"

"But you'll remember it, and that's the important thing. Just as I'll remember the sight of you, *chérie*. You have the loveliest body I have ever seen, soft and feminine and— "

"Let me go, please," she whispered, although he wasn't even touching her, except with his mind and his eyes. But he stood back a pace, and as if she was released from some magical hold, Tania stepped downwards into the water, not gingerly as she normally did, letting the water lap her carefully at first, but walking straight down into it. Gasping a little at the shock of its coolness in contrast to the hot sun, her breasts held buoyantly by the water for a moment, she plunged into its caressing balm.

Almost at the same moment, she heard the sound of Claude's athletic body slicing into the water, and while Tania still bobbed up and down to adjust herself to the new environment, Clause was already striking past her, his powerful arms scything effortlessly, as much at home here as on the side of a mountain. Tania lifted her feet from the bottom of the pool and struck out in the other direction. The water cooled and caressed her cheeks. It was sheer bliss to feel the hot sun on her head, and yet feel part of this new liquid warmth.

She turned onto her back, floating luxuriously, her long chestnut hair fanning out like burnished gold before it became saturated, clinging to her shoulders in mermaid strands. Her eyes momentarily closed.

Her hands idly paddled at her sides, keeping her afloat, when suddenly she was caught in another pair of arms, and her eyes were wide open at once. Claude's face was a whisper away from hers. At the contact, Tania's legs plunged downwards, treading water, but his arms held her tight. She could feel the rippling sinews of his forearms as her hands automatically closed around them.

Droplets of pearly water clung to his dark hair and the bronze of his skin. He was like some dark pagan god, the irrational thought swept through her mind. If this was another ploy to embrace her, Tania didn't think much of it. All she wanted was to enjoy a swim without Claude's disturbing presence. Even as she thought it and was angered by it, his legs wrapped themselves around hers, entwining with hers, so that they resembled one person. She was acutely conscious of his flesh against hers beneath the water, and the fact that the tiny scraps of fabric separating them were hopelessly inadequate for disguising his desire for her. Tania burned with fury, refusing to allow the flame of an answering desire to invade every part of her.

"Let me go." She kept her voice as steady as she could, considering she was shaking with rage, and something else.

"I will, now that you're not drifting straight for the side of the pool," Claude said, close to her mouth. "I could hardly ignore the fact that you'd have given your head a crack if you'd gone on dog-paddling the way you were."

Tania turned her head sharply, seeing that she had gone perilously near the side of the pool from the middle. It was easy to drift along, lulled by the sun and the blue water. She felt her rage dispel, feeling suddenly foolish.

"Thank you," she said jerkily, still entwined in his powerful hold. "I think I can manage by myself now."

She wanted to be out of his arms, she thought desperately, before he was too aware of the way he rioted through her senses. Even if he didn't hold her physically, he still had a stranglehold on her emotional reactions, and right now, he was holding her very, very physically. If the pool water hadn't cooled her down, Tania was certain she would be breaking out in beads of perspiration by now. As it was, her heart raced, and she was sure Claude must know it, feel it, next to his . . .

"The feel of you in my arms is the most exciting thing to happen to me in a long time," his voice was husky-rough. "The feel and the scent of you, and the way you fit against my skin as if God fashioned you for me alone. You've started a fever in me, Tania, *chérie*, that only you can cure. Will you be my medication, my lovely girl?"

The sudden tremor that ran through her at his words was smothered by his lips tasting hers in sweet salty kisses. While her thoughts whirled somewhere in space, his head lowered slightly, moving downwards beneath the water, to rest against her throat, her breasts, the soft roundness of her stomach . . . Tania gasped wordlessly at the erotic sensations his mouth was awakening in her.

The sudden sound of childish laughter brought her back to her senses. Was Claude mad, to behave this way? He loosed his hold on her at once as she began to struggle, shooting smoothly away from her beneath the water, to emerge at the far side of the pool just as Alphonse appeared through the tall trees with Henri, exuberantly calling out to his uncle.

Minutes later, Tania wondered if the brief seduction had really taken place, or if she had imagined it. Once the child joined them, Claude was a different man, no longer the prowling tiger with her as his prey, but the considerate caring uncle. Tania spluttered the water from her eyes and mouth when she had swam away from the others for a few moments of recovery, treading water at the deep end of the pool, as she watched Claude prepare Henri for his entry into the water.

Her throat thickened a little. The boy was so thin in his swimming trunks, the arm bands to keep him afloat looking incongruously large. Despite the exercises he did every day, his legs looked wasted through lack of normal childish activity, and the thickening in Tania's throat became a lump of sympathy as Claude towelled himself off quickly so as not to chill Henri all at once. Then he lifted his nephew bodily out of the wheelchair and stepped gently into the shallow end of the pool with Henri in his arms.

It was clear that the child trusted Claude implicitly. There was no fear of being dipped into the water too quickly, or of being forced out of his depth, or left to battle alone until he was ready. Tania could only admire the infinite patience with which Claude instructed Henri, waiting for him to flex the pale limbs and test his own strength, before he finally managed a crazy dog-paddle with Claude giving him as much encouragement as if he'd swum the English Channel and back again.

"Watch me, Tania," Henri squealed out to her as his arms flailed about. She smiled back at him, glad that the droplets of water on her face and body hid the shine of tears in her eyes at that moment. Henri mustn't see them. Not when such a small thing as flailing about in a private pool was such a personal triumph to him. Tania sensed that all the fierce Girard pride was instilled in Henri every bit as forcefully as in Claude. He wouldn't want to see pity in her eyes.

All the same, the sight of Claude being so gentle and attentive to the boy was oddly moving, far more so than she had expected it to be. She was well aware of his love for Henri, but this particular way of showing it was unbearably poignant to her. She could still hear the ring of passion and frustration in Claude's voice when he had told her he'd give Henri the mountains if he could. They were just words, but what Tania was seeing now was love.

She decided to sunbathe after a while, drying herself off with the towel while Claude still watched over Henri in the pool. He must have been aware of her movements, however, because he called to her to use some of the lotion he'd brought for her skin. It was far better than her proprietary stuff, he told her. It was in a bag near her lounger, and Tania smoothed its soothing liquid over every exposed part of her. A good tan would be an added bonus of being here, she thought. She may as well make the most of it. She was glad that Claude was still in the pool with Henri. She didn't want any offers of help to smoothe the lotion into her skin.

She lay back with a sigh of pure pleasure when she was done. The sun and the lotion pampered her skin. If Claude's fingers hadn't been the ones to caress the protective oil into it, she had the strangest sensation of knowing exactly how they would have felt. Strong, sensitive, kneading her flesh until it was pliant and supple, responding to whatever he wanted of her.

Tania moved restlessly on the lounger. The splashing of the water, and the occasional soft breeze and the two voices, one young, one deeply mature, were having a hypnotic effect on her. And despite the suntan lotion, she knew it would be foolish to stay in the sun for too long this first day. Her English skin was unused to its fierce rays, and it felt far hotter than usual to her touch. She would be wise to go indoors soon and take a refreshing shower. It was siesta time.

"I'm going in now, Claude," she called out. "I've had enough for one day."

He smiled at her, and she hoped he wouldn't make any fatuous remark at that moment. He didn't. Instead, he scooped Henri up in his arms again, where the boy clung to his neck. They rose out of the shallow end together, and from the awkward angle, Claude's limp that was normally barely noticeable to Tania, was more evident again. So too were the scars running down the back of one leg, grim reminders of the gashes he had suffered on the mountain. Tania hadn't seen them before, but the sight of the weals brought James vividly back to her mind again.

How soon before all this harmonious, elegant château life was disrupted for the excitement and the danger that Claude and James had exulted in so much? How long before another climb was organised, a dangerous rescue mission undertaken, and the women left behind would know the mental torture that accompanied every expedition? A shudder ran through her, and she gathered up her towel and her coverall, sliding it over her head, and left the other two together. She could have offered to dry Henri's small body, as Claude was gently doing now, but she thought they would prefer to continue their daily ritual. They would prefer to be alone, as she did too . . .

Within a week, Tania's body was tanned to a deep golden brown. It was impossible to keep away from the enticing pool, but on other days, Madame joined them at the poolside in a light summer dress and shady hat. Several days Monique didn't go to the boutique in Toulouse, and

91

made it a more relaxing family party. Relaxing for Tania, without the too intimate ambience produced when she and Claude were there alone before Alphonse brought the boy to join them.

She suspected Claude waited for the exact moment she left her room. She suspected too that he gave Alphonse instructions to let Mademoiselle have ten minutes alone in the pool before the child's exercises began. Only to Claude, that meant being alone with him. No matter how often Tania varied the time, the little tête-à-tête continued.

By now she tried to ignore the implications that Claude was determined to be alone with her when he could, in as intimate a way as possible. In the mornings they worked together, and the outline of the book was slowly taking shape, though there was a vast amount to be done. Some of the time, Claude's own affairs took up his time, when Tania was free to wander around the lovely grounds of the château, and to take coffee with Madame Girard.

"The French air suits you, my dear," the older woman told her with a smile one afternoon. "You look even more like your brother with that healthy outdoor glow in your cheeks. I think you should stay here always." She spoke with the complacent air of one who could always do whatever she wished. Tania laughed out loud.

"I can't possibly do that, Madame."

"Why not? Who is to stop you? You have no family, no ties – unless there is a young man in England. Forgive me if I become too enthusiastic, Tania, but I have grown very fond of you, and we Girards are a mite selfish at times. We forget that people have other lives to lead."

Tania shook her head. "There's no young man in England, Madame. At least, not in the way you mean.

I'm not in love with him." Maybe she had needed this distance between herself and David to see that the luke-warm affection she felt for him could never in her wildest dreams be compared with love. There was no tumultuous spinning of her senses whenever she thought of him; no charge of electricity whenever they touched, spoke, glanced across a room towards each other; no wanton pleasuring of her mind and body whenever his dark eyes told her that he wanted her, desired her . . . She caught herself up short. David's eyes were blue, not dark velvet brown.

"Then what is to prevent you staying?" Madame went on practically. "If your pride will not let you stay as my permanent guest, then take on more fully the English teaching with Henri. Already, we have to be discreet when we lapse into your language, which is to your credit, my dear. He loves you, as we all do. I was quite sure we would. We all loved James, you see."

Such simple words from this well-bred woman made them all the more sincere. Tania still fumbled for something to say. It just wasn't possible. She had her job in London. Claude hadn't bought her completely. Remembering the outrageous way he had gone to Lance Hillman and bought her time here, roused the sanity in her once more.

"It's just not possible, Madame."

"There is always another way to persuade her, Mother." Claude's lazy voice made them both jump. Neither had heard him moving towards them where they sat outside on the patio, drinking iced coffee in the late afternoon. He poured himself a cup, his eyes challenging Tania as he continued.

"She could always marry me!"

Tania's heart jolted. She was unable to tear her eyes away from his indolent stare for a few seconds. She felt the heat in her face, and the erratic beat of her heart. It was said with no more feeling than the way he would order some new item for his amusement, and Madame admonished him at once.

"Claude, really! That is no way to propose to a lovely young lady! It's insulting to toss such an offer into the conversation like that. Take no notice of him, Tania. He can be really crass when he chooses."

"I wouldn't dream of taking it seriously, Madame," she declared, her voice oddly brittle.

Claude isn't the marrying kind . . . she seemed to hear James's voice telling her. *More than one girl thought she was destined to be the mother of the Girard future generation, and inherit the family fortune, but it will have to be someone very special to make Claude give up his bachelor status. He's having too good a time. Why should he settle for one, when he can have them all . . . ?*

James's words were very clear in Tania's head at that moment. At the time, Tania hadn't really heeded them. She had certainly not been aware of the extent of the Girard family fortune. They had just been words spoken cheekily by her brother, tossed into the conversation like pebbles in a lake, the way Madame Girard had just referred to Claude's marriage offer to her. It wasn't meant to be heeded either. It was an insult, just as she had said.

All the same, it was the first proposal Tania had received in her life, despite the fact that David Lee was slowly working around to it. No man who loved a woman as she wanted, needed to be loved, should take so long to get around to it, the thought skidded into her mind.

94

The sudden turbulence in her veins as she caught the quizzical, mocking look on Claude's face alarmed her. She was conscious of several emotions at once. Anger at the insult, puzzlement, disappointment . . . though why she should be disappointed, she couldn't explain. A feeling of wild, explosive joy, tempered with a fatalistic refusal to admit he could ever have meant her to take his proposal seriously. A brief, momentary question in her mind as to his reaction if she did . . .

"I apologise, *chérie*," Claude was saying gravely, his voice neutral. "Next time it will be done in the appropriate manner, all moonlight and roses."

"Do stop it, Claude," Madame began to laugh, clearly thinking he was teasing Tania to the point of embarrassment. "It's the middle of the day now, and Tania's too sensible to bother with your nonsense. And the roses are already fading."

It seemed like an ominous remark. The patio was surrounded by rose bushes in full bloom, their scent heady and overpowering in the afternoon heat.

"Then if Tania won't have me, perhaps we should throw a party, Mother, and I can surround myself with pretty girls to console myself," he said lightly. "It's not such a bad idea. Monique may even get around to deciding it's time she married Denis after all. And I shall recover from my broken heart."

Madame still laughed, not hearing the little edge in his voice, that to Tania spelt far more than the casual words he said. Claude Girard wasn't used to being rejected in any way. The proposal was no more than a silly remark, but she had turned down his sexual advances with cold English scorn, and that was an affront to his pride.

A cool little breeze blew across the patio, scattering

95

the petals of the full-blown roses in a soft carpet of pink about their feet, before they were carried over the smooth green lawns. Their movements filled Tania with a strange, throat-catching sadness.

Chapter 6

Tania had expected the work with Claude to be a strain on her emotions. The continual references to James, which was her reason for being here, was not easy on her nerves, and she couldn't avoid them. Reliving the formative past when she and James were children, and having the later years filled in by Claude, by photos, letters, newspaper cuttings, the frequent reminiscences of Madame Girard and Monique, were all guaranteed to make the experience supercharged for Tania. More so than she had expected, because Claude's demanding personality was more disturbing than she had anticipated.

She had been prepared to meet as much antagonism from him as she gave, and sometimes she got it. At other times, she found it impossible to read the expression in his eyes, or to know when he was mocking her or being serious. Physically, she could never be unaware of him as a man, in every sense of the word, and subtly, her opinions of him were changing.

She didn't want them to change, she thought in a panic. She wanted to hold on to her image of him as the danger-seeking, reckless playboy, but she knew she was losing her grip on her long-held impressions. Firstly, she was forced to admit that Claude was a very caring man. That much was evident in his dealings with

Henri. His heart grieved for the child, and Tania never doubted that.

Then, too, she discovered that he poured his own money into the mountain rescue work, which would come into full prominence later in the year when the winter season began. In a month or two, the first snows on the favoured slopes of the mountains would attract experts and novices, and all the skills of Claude's hand-picked teams would be called upon.

She learned that the climbs that had made Claude and James famous as fearless mountaineers, were often sponsored for charity, or made to provide new, detailed routes for the less experienced to follow. He was really a good guy, Tania told herself cynically.

But the cynicism usually faded, because as her opinions of Claude changed, so did her feelings towards him, and that was something else she wouldn't allow to happen. She wouldn't let herself fall under his spell as so many other women had done. She didn't want to be one of his "good times". She could be as fiercely demanding as he when it came to wanting love. And she would demand exclusive rights, to be loved passionately and wantonly, as long as it was a one-man, one-woman love, and Claude's casual offer of marriage was as shaming to her as it was meaningless.

Naturally, he had never expected her to accept. It would just serve him right, Tania thought, her amber eyes suddenly gleaming, if she were to pretend to take him seriously, and take him up on it . . . if she dared. But taking chances had never been her forte. She left that to men like Claude and James. The idea left her mind the second it occurred to her.

As if to reassure herself that this episode in her life

was only temporary, she wrote long letters to friends in England, and looked forward eagerly to the replies. David Lee wrote long, ponderous letters a little like himself, though always ending with the hope that she'd be coming home soon. Lance sent her brief, businesslike notes, included with the longer, more garrulous epics from his wife. Tania wrote to one of the girls in her department a couple of times, but got only the briefest letter back, and didn't bother again.

Outside the company, she realised suddenly how few friends she had. She *was* practically a recluse! Where were all the vivacious young women with whom she had shared the school years in Paris? She answered her own question. Spread about the world, successful in careers as she was successful, or married with children, secure in their own particular heavens.

Claude, on the contrary, was obviously all set to prove just how many friends and acquaintances he had. This was clear to Tania as she came across Madame Girard sealing a great pile of invitations one afternoon when she had had her swim, and left Claude and Henri at the pool.

"You'll love our parties, Tania," Madame greeted her. "Many of Claude's friends were friends of James too, and will be longing to meet you."

"I'll do my best not to let you down, then. I'm not very good at parties, I'm afraid."

"A pretty girl like you? I cannot believe it. We are all very informal here, Tania. Just relax and enjoy yourself. If you want a new dress, I'm sure Monique would be happy to bring you a selection from her boutique, or you may like to go there one afternoon. I'm sure Claude would drive you."

"I'll see," she murmured. She hadn't brought anything

too spectacular for partywear, and she didn't want to appear the little English mouse. She knew she was talking herself into buying something new, and Madame had evidently mentioned it to Claude, because he told her he wanted to go into Toulouse himself the following week, two days before the party, and he'd be happy to take her to Monique's establishment.

She could hardly refuse, even though she would have been more comfortable out of Claude's company for a little while. She watched his strong tanned hands on the wheel of the car, and wondered just why he disturbed her so much. Why did she sometimes lie sleepless in the warm sultry night, her windows open, and wonder if he was doing the same in the room next to hers? She imagined him there sometimes, not willingly, but as if it was a compulsion within her.

Did he sometimes gaze out of the bedroom window as she did, to where the dark hazy mass of the mountains rose dizzily towards the sky? Did he have trouble sleeping, as she suspected, from the occasional sounds of his feet padding around the room late at night, the rustle of pages being turned in a book, the click of his bedside light? Did he lie, sleepless, eyes staring unseeingly at the ceiling, lonely in the night?

"Are you all right?" Claude glanced at her as he steered the car around the bends in the road, hearing her small indrawn breath. "You're very quiet today."

She sought the first refuge she could think of, as if afraid that he would guess that her palms were damp, imagining for one heart-stopping moment that she had been the one to go to him, to erase his loneliness, to slide beneath the soft warm cocoon of his bedcovers and enter the embrace of those waiting arms . . .

"I'm not good at parties. I told your mother as much." Her voice was jerky, stilted. The thoughts churned in her mind. Was it solely a male preserve to feel this sudden surge of desire that was erupting inside her with all the force of an electrical storm? It was a feeling Tania had never met before. Not this strong, this mind-stunning, this wonderful. Was this the surprise of love, that it hit you between the eyes so blindingly that it knocked you off-balance and rendered you almost speechless?

She didn't love him. *Couldn't* love him. He was the enemy. Words swam in and out of her senses in little staccato bursts, machine-gun fast. It was useless to love him. Wasted. He loved too many women. Too many. She had to be the only one . . .

"Don't be ridiculous, Tania. It's only children who are scared of parties. Just because you're scared of life, don't hide away from everything it has to offer!" He was indulgent. He spoke to her the way he spoke to Henri, gently chiding.

Angry at him, suddenly vulnerable and defenceless in her new awareness, she said, "I'm not afraid of life. Just because I don't match up to your idea of James's sister, don't belittle me because I think differently from him – or you. Not everyone enjoys the senseless prattle of party small-talk."

If she was being rude, she didn't care. He would be angry in return. She mentally braced herself for a verbal attack.

Instead, he spoke abruptly. "What makes you think you don't match up to anyone? You need have no worries at all at the party, if that's what you're afraid of. Nobody else will hold a candle to you."

If it was meant to be a compliment, it didn't sound

like it. It was too clinical, with none of Claude's usual sexual undertones. From any other man, Tania might have taken the words at face value and accepted with a little glow that they meant exactly what they said. She had extreme difficulty in applying those rules to Claude. She was too suspicious of his motives. She kept stubbornly silent, rather than be drawn into further comment, and was vastly relieved when the town of Toulouse came into view, and Claude stopped the car outside a small and exclusive little boutique.

"I'll be back for you in an hour or so," he said, proving that he really did have business in the town. "Monique will no doubt offer you coffee or cognac, as she does to all her valued clients. Until then, have fun."

He reached for her hand, putting it to his lips before she could stop him. His kiss tingled on the back of her hand, vibrantly warm. Tania got out of the car quickly, feeling the hot sun on her back immediately. Not quite so strong now though. The seasons were changing, and it suited her English temperament better. Claude waved goodbye, and she pushed open the door of the boutique.

It was instantly obvious that this was no cheap-jack store! She wondered how on earth she could afford any of the lovely gowns displayed on the plastic models. Madame should have warned her. She was an English working girl, not one of the Paris jet-set! Monique came to greet her with the formal handshake of the French, her face smiling readily. Tania liked Claude's sister very much, and decided it was best to be frank with her. Monique waved aside all her protests.

"My mother insists that you have anything you wish, Tania. It is her gift to you for agreeing to Claude's rough-shod methods in getting you to the château. He is very forceful, my brother, and this work you do with him must be painful at times. Please don't be offended, Tania. My mother loves to be generous, and she is very fond of you."

How could she refuse when it was said so graciously? It was a heady experience to be shown so many lovely creations, and know she could choose whatever she liked. She settled for a beautiful cocktail dress in glowing bronze. The neckline was low and sensuously exciting. The material clung softly to her curves, flaring out to a swirling skirt from a tiny waist. The bronze fabric was threaded with gleaming slivers of gold, and the entire effect was a perfect foil to her honeyed complexion and amber eyes, which were arrestingly complemented by the stunning dress.

"It's absolutely right for you," Monique said enviously. "It's perfect. Claude will love you in it."

Tania's eyes blurred a little as she went back to the fitting-room to change into her blouse and skirt once more. Would he love her in the dress? It wasn't said with any deep meaning intended. It was just an expression people used. It was only now, as she held the lovely fabric in her hands, that Tania knew how much she wished the words could be true. And only now that she realised she had chosen the dress because she was seeing its effect through Claude's eyes. Wanting to be beautiful for him. No-one else mattered.

She combed through her long hair with trembling hands. It was all happening too soon, too fast, too much a reversal of all her earlier aversion towards him. The thin line between hating and loving had been crossed over so effortlessly, she still felt totally bewildered by it. And just as totally determined not to let him know it. She couldn't bear it if he ever guessed that she was not as immune to him as she pretended. It hadn't been pretence until now. But now that the feelings seemed to be exploding inside her, Tania admitted that they had been slowly growing for some time. Like the roses, they had suddenly blossomed into glorious life, though why she should think of roses at that moment, she couldn't think. And then she knew.

The roses had been caught by the breeze on the patio when Claude had made his remark about her marrying him in order to stay at the château. Had he meant it to sound that mercenary, she thought now? New meanings to everything he said or did burned into her consciousness. She blotted them all out, as Monique called to her that coffee was waiting for her in the salon of the boutique. But she couldn't quite blot out the sweet fragrant scent of the roses.

By the time Claude called for her, Tania was acutely sensitive to every move he made. She noted the affectionate smile between him and his sister, and the easy relationship they had. She and James had never known anything so comfortable.

She noticed the way his clothes fitted and moulded his masculine shape. She noted the grace with which he moved, the lithe, athletic walk, the proud tilt of his head, the arrogance in his eyes that could soften into tenderness. She remembered the sharp inexplicable envy she had felt when he had held Henri in his arms that first day at the pool. And now she knew exactly the reason. This was love. This irrational, sometimes dizzying, sometimes overwhelming feeling. It was love. Love.

"Did you have a good day?" Claude asked her as they drove away from Toulouse, glancing at her with a smile.

Had the timbre of his voice always been that deep, that sexy? Or was it only that her ears were suddenly hyper-sensitive to the fact?

"Marvellous," she said quickly. "It's always a boost to buy something new, especially the knock-out dress I bought. I didn't realise Monique's boutique would be so exciting."

"I can't wait to see this creation." Claude was grinning now. "If it's as good as you say, I'll have to blindfold every other man in the room."

"Why? Do you think I'm your exclusive property?" Tania said, before she could stop herself. A crazy reckless need to hurt him rose up in her. If he *could* be hurt. "Why shouldn't I look around for some eligible Frenchman, since I'm obliged to stay here for your rescarches? I might find myself married to a count— "

She gasped as Claude's hand suddenly reached out and gripped her arm. He was driving too fast around the narrow bends in the road, and she knew what a foolish time she had chosen to goad him in this way.

"Don't play with me, Tania. It doesn't suit you to be so flippant about serious matters."

"Put both hands on the wheel, please." She could hardly concentrate on anything else at that moment, as the car tore around the hairpin bends. Was he trying to kill them both?

"Then tell me you didn't mean what you just said," he spoke grimly, not relenting for a second.

"I don't see why I should," she muttered, "but if it will stop your stupid showing off, then all right. I didn't mean what I said. I've no intention of look-ing for a husband at your party, or anywhere else.

105

And certainly not a French husband!" She finished with heavy sarcasm. "I prefer my men to act a little more civilised."

Claude let go, and she rubbed at her arm. He hadn't really hurt her, but the pressure of his fingers was like a brand on her skin. She glanced at his set face. It looked as if it was carved out of marble. Tania was filled with misery. She had just discovered that she loved him, and here they were, like two enemies on the battlefield once more. Love didn't enter into Claude's vocabulary, she thought bitterly. Substitute desire, possession, lust, but it wasn't love he wanted from her.

"Like your pale Englishman, I suppose?" he retorted. "The one who sends you so many letters and has to print his name so laboriously on the back of the envelope. Does he think you'll have forgotten him unless he does so?" He was scathing, contemptuous of David. Perversely, Tania rallied to his defence.

"At least he knows when to take no for an answer," she said heatedly. "He doesn't storm his way into a woman's emotions by caveman methods."

"Then he is a poor example of a man," Claude whipped back. "He obviously can't want a woman enough. I never take no for an answer."

The arrogant conceit of him took Tania's breath away. How could she think that she loved him, even for a moment, she raged? Thank goodness the crazy emotions were subsiding. With his own words, he had killed them. She didn't love him after all. She definitely didn't. She deliberately shifted a few inches away from him in the small sports car and stared out of the window without speaking to him again for the rest of the journey. She was incensed to think he had studied her letters and knew how many she had received from David. He had no right, no right at all.

When they arrived at the château, lovely in the late afternoon sun, the shadows already lengthening, Tania reached into the rear seat for the dress box without a word. Claude reached for it too, and his hand closed over hers. She met his eyes, angry glints darkening the amber.

"I can manage," she said frigidly. "I'm not made of glass."

"I'm beginning to wonder if you're made of flesh and blood," Claude said shortly, his own eyes snapping at her. "Am I not to see the dress until the party, then?"

Tania shook her head. A sudden weepy feeling took hold of her. The moments when she had worn the bronze dress in the boutique had been so magical, knowing she wore it for only him. Now, she wished he never had to see it at all. Everything had changed. Nothing would be quite the same again.

"It's to be a surprise," she mumbled. His fingers moved slightly on her bare skin, caressing, gentle.

"Don't fight me, Tania," he said. "Be my friend, as James was my friend."

She looked at him wordlessly. And then the words came out in a gasping torrent.

"I can't. I don't think I can ever be your friend. I always knew it. Why couldn't you have left me alone? I never wanted to meet you – never. Why didn't you leave me to live my own life? I didn't ask to become part of yours. James knew that. At least he respected it."

She could see by his shocked face that he took her words to mean her hatred of James's obsession with the mountains, and Claude's encouragement of it. It was what she hoped he would think. Anything but the truth, that mere friendship was something that could never exist between them. It had to be all or nothing. Love or hate. There could be no compromise. And she would settle for nothing less than love from him. Total, exclusive love.

She was learning more about herself by the minute, Tania thought painfully. She was every bit as bad as Claude. She wanted what he wanted. Exclusive rights. But for her there had to be that one vital extra ingredient. There had to be love.

She pulled the box from the car and almost ran inside the château. Madame Girard was in the drawing-room. Tania hesitated. She must thank her for the lovely gift, but right now she felt her cheeks were too heated, her eyes too bright, to be due to a shopping expedition, however exciting. She would take the dress to her room, and take a shower, inviting Madame to see the dress later. She turned quickly to ask Claude to relay as much to his mother, and was surprised to see a look of something akin to anguish in his dark eyes. He just couldn't believe he was being turned down, Tania thought cynically. It was probably a novelty to him, and one that he didn't like. It wouldn't hurt him to share the feelings of the common herd for once!

By the evening of the party, Tania had her feelings more or less under control. They had to be. In her job, she had been trained not to betray any hint of emotion at some of the odd phrases the foreign delegates put to her. She mustn't laugh or scoff, or appear to be superior when they struggled with her language. She must be calm at all times, and put them at their ease. Such training stood her in good stead now, when the last thing she wanted was to betray her feelings to Claude.

108

If she had expected his pursual of her to continue, she was in for a shock. The party guests were clearly in the same social scale as the Girards, if not all as wealthy. They glittered, sparkled, with bright, frothy conversation. They were young, witty, successful. They adored Claude, and Tania realised she was just another party guest. She hadn't really wanted to be anything else, but she was slightly piqued that Claude treated her so.

There was one special moment though, before any of the guests had arrived. Madame Girard had seen the glittery bronze dress by now, and Tania thanked her warmly for it. But until the evening of the party, no-one but Monique had seen Tania wearing it. They insisted laughingly that she made an entrance. To her embarrassment, the entire family waited at the foot of the curving staircase as she came down.

Her one consolation was that she knew she looked her best. She had never felt so regal, so gorgeously attired as she did that night. And as if to complement the gown, Tania knew that her hair shone like burnished chestnut, her skin glowed. She held the banister lightly with pink-manicured fingers as her delicate high heels trod carefully on the twisting stairs.

There were only five people awaiting her, yet it seemed as if a sea of faces looked her way as she reached the bottom. Madame, pleased and smiling; Monique, splendid in a sheath of black silk, the distinguished Denis by her side; Henri, allowed to stay up for an hour or so, struck dumb at the golden vision in front of him, and Claude.

He moved towards her, and then there was only one face that she saw. He wore a black evening suit and bow tie, a crisp white silk shirt accentuating the deep tan of his skin and the dark hair and eyes. His look was enigmatic as he approached her, to take her cool hands in his and kiss each one separately, deliberately, as if he had no conception of how his touch inflamed her. Nor could he, from her serene exterior. Only inside did her blood surge more wildly, her nerve-ends tingle and curl, her pulse race.

"You are the most beautiful woman in the world," Claude said, his voice very low so that only she could hear. "You take my breath away. I would give you my heart, if you had not already broken it into little pieces."

The flamboyant, extravagant words were interrupted by Henri's shrill voice.

"Are you a princess, Tania? You look like the one in my story-book."

Tania laughed quickly, moving away from Claude's mesmeric gaze to give him a quick kiss on the cheek.

"Thank you, darling. That's the nicest thing anyone has ever said to me."

Not quite, but right now she was thankful the child had broken the electric tension between herself and Claude at that moment. She had felt it instantly, even if no-one else seemed aware of it. But she deliberately kept away from Claude as much as she could during the evening, once he had introduced her to people. She had no wish to be seen as the little English *ingénue*, unable to hold an intelligent conversation. And the party guests were pleasantly surprised to find Tania could converse fluently in their own language, and had no need to practise their varying levels of English on her.

She danced, she conversed, she enjoyed herself – more than she had expected to. Henri was put to bed under protest, and she agreed to go up with him for a short while, since he couldn't bear to let go of his golden princess. She came back downstairs in time to catch a snippet of conversation between several guests below.

"Well, I know she's James Paget's sister, but how long is she staying? Do you think she's Claude's latest? I never thought he'd fall for an English girl, though I must admit she's very charming, and beautiful too."

"Since when did it matter to Claude which flag they were born under, *chérie*? A woman is a woman, and that one is definitely all woman."

Tania's cheeks burned. She couldn't have avoided hearing the conversation, and while some women might think it complimentary, she hated to hear herself compared with some of Claude's past loves, as if they were all in some kind of cattle-market. Her poise wavered, but the guests moved away from the stairs before she reached the foot, and didn't notice her. Her eyes smarted with unshed tears that she would be too proud to show, anyway. The party was in full swing. She wondered if she could sneak away to her room, and if anyone would miss her. Before she could decide, a shadow blocked her vision, and Claude was holding out his arms to her.

Dancing with Claude was sweet torture, but Tania could hardly refuse. Couples drifted past them, wrapped in each others' arms as they moved to the seductive music, in worlds of their own. Tania's world was very different to any of theirs. Hers was one of magic laced with pain. *To Claude, a woman is a woman . . .* That other guest's words seemed to drum into her mind, reminding her that none of this was real. Not the brush of Claude's lips against her cheek, nor his soft-whispered words, nor the feel of him next to her, so close it seemed they shared mutual heartbeats.

It was all a game. Ironic, when it was he who kept telling

111

her not to play games with him. His game was a far more dangerous one than hers. It undermined all the carefully built fabric of her life. That veneer behind which she hid, that protected her from the wider world that spelt danger. Danger that had killed her parents and her brother . . . She shuddered briefly in Claude's arms. He felt the tremor run through her and his arms tightened.

"Do you believe in fate, *chérie*?" he asked softly.

She was wary. "If you mean, do I believe that everything is pre-ordained, then I'm honestly not sure. I do believe that we can change our fate, that we have the God-given right to choose. Otherwise we would all be puppets, wouldn't we?"

"Then if you believe that we can change our fate, you must believe in it," he went on, smooth as silk. He pressed her even closer to him, his body becoming almost part of hers as she seemed to curve against his hard masculine frame in one fluid movement. "So believe in *us*, Tania."

"Us? There is no *us*," she spoke through dry lips. She refused to be one of his women. She heard him give a soft laugh, the sound richly vibrant against her breasts.

"Then what are you doing here, in my house, in my arms, in my life? You said it yourself. You have the God-given right to choose, and you chose to come here. Why won't you accept that you are my fate, as I am yours?"

"I didn't exactly choose to come, did I?" He may seduce her with his caressing hands on her body that seemed to burn through the silky bronze fabric of her dress to touch her skin with fire. He may touch her cheek with his mouth, so near to her lips that she felt she would scream for him to reach them. He may dissolve her into melting fire by his animal masculinity . . . but he wasn't getting away with that!

She moved slightly out of his arms as best she could, though she was still imprisoned by them, and the other party guests dancing around them. They didn't exist for Tania. They were mere watercolours on the edge of her vision as the bright dresses moved past. There was only Claude's dark face, still smiling, not in the least upset by her words, which made him all the more dangerous. When he was angry, she could hit back. Smiling, seductively sure of himself, she didn't trust him an inch.

"I couldn't have forced you against your will, Tania. Nor could I have forced your boss to give you the time off, despite my offer to buy it. Admit that fate had a hand in it. Admit that you're not exactly indifferent to me, when everything about you tells me otherwise!"

She despised him for his arrogance. It was as if he knew exactly when her feelings towards him had changed. Knew when to close in for the kill. Her heart raced, then steadied with a sudden strange calm. Desperately, she knew that there was only one way out for her, and that was to get away from here. She was aware of her own weakness where Claude was concerned. That much she would admit. It would only be a matter of time before he overcame all her resistance, became her lover. The sweetness of the thought made her dizzy for a moment, as if the ground shifted slightly beneath her feet. But what then? When he had had his fill of her, would she be relegated like all the others? To become just one of the legion of others in his life? She couldn't bear that. Far better to get out now.

Chapter 7

She told him the next morning, when the party guests had all gone, and the château was back to its normal elegant appearance, cleared up by an army of silent workers, so that by the time the family appeared for a late breakfast, it was just like any other day. Yet not the same at all.

Yesterday's sunlit warmth had gone, and a heavy mist lay over the valley. The chill of autumn was in the air, and the change in the weather matched Tania's mood. She had spent a restless night, her mind too alert after the party to sleep, and now she had a dull headache. But when Claude said he was going to spend an hour or so in his study, looking not unlike the way she felt, Tania said immediately that she would join him there. Henri was still complaining at missing most of the party, and his mother promised to take a day off from the boutique, and she and Madame would take him out when the mist cleared a little.

"There's no need for you to work today," Claude said curtly to Tania. "You must be tired."

All his warmth seemed to have vanished too, but she wouldn't be fooled by it. "I'm here to work. I prefer it."

"Come with us, Tania," Henri pleaded. "Don't go into Claude's stuffy old study!"

114

She laughed at him. "You go and enjoy yourself, darling. I'll see you later."

She didn't feel like eating much breakfast anyway. She had too many things on her mind. She wondered if Claude had anticipated what she was going to say. In the study he sat behind his desk as if it was a stage prop, though the simile was one that would never be applied to Claude. He would never need such an aid to get him through an interview. All the same, he sat there unsmiling, as if his face was sculpted out of stone, and for a breathless moment, Tania longed to go to him, to touch the hard, tight skin around his mouth, to kiss away the tension, to bring the warmth back to his eyes . . . she pushed the feeling down at once.

"I've decided to go back to England as soon as it's convenient, Claude," she spoke in a rush, before she lost her nerve. Though why should she be suddenly afraid of him? He didn't own her. She was free to do whatever she wanted. She ignored the fact that her palms were clammy, her heartbeats loud in her ears. The blood pounded there, rushing, like the sound of the sea over a shingle beach. She was angry with herself for reacting like a frightened child in front of a headmaster, but that was just how Claude made her feel at that moment.

"It's far from convenient," he said, in a hard voice. "We've barely begun here." He gestured to the piles of notes they had started to assemble. She wouldn't be swayed.

"I'm sorry. I've given you sufficient to get a clear picture of James's early years. I hadn't anticipated that you would want me to help write the book. I thought you merely wanted background information. If there's anything further I can tell you, I'm sure I can send it to you from London."

He stared at her, unsmiling, not speaking. His gaze seemed to penetrate her very bones. It unnerved her. It wasn't sexual so much as possessive at that moment, telling her potently that she should not, could not, do this. That she belonged here, to him, for as long as he wanted her. The message he sent out was as clear as if he had shouted it from the rooftops. She flinched back from it. Nobody owned her, nor ever would.

"You don't need me, Claude." Her voice was more resolute, dragged past the dryness in her throat that she wouldn't let him sense. She held her chin high. "You can manage perfectly well without me— "

His fist slammed down on the desk so hard and so fast, Tania gave a little gasp of alarm. It was as if he had struck *her*. She felt the pain of contact as sharply as if he'd rammed the fist into her face. She stepped back a pace as he stood up. He didn't move away from the desk, and outlined against the dense mist outside the window, she had the impression of a dark devil surrounded by swirling vapour. If she had been unnerved before, she was doubly so now.

"I need you," he grated. "Haven't you been listening to a word I've said all this time? *I* need you. Henri needs you. James needs you— "

"James is dead." The pricking behind her eyelids as she mouthed the words made her swallow. He was despicable, using weapons against which she was helpless. Why did he do this to her? Was she the only woman in the world who could sate his vanity right now? Did he need her so badly to add to his collection?

"It's because James is dead that I need you," he said

116

coldly. "I need your help. You know that. But if your feelings aren't as filial as you would have me believe, and since you obviously care nothing about my needs, then what of Henri? The child has grown very fond of you. He is making excellent progress with his English, because he wants to please you so much."

"There are proper tutors who would do as well. Don't use Henri as a kind of blackmail," she said angrily. "First James, and now the boy. Are you proud of yourself for your devious methods of getting a woman to stay with you? I'm surprised you resort to such crudity. It's hardly subtle, is it?"

He was around the desk so fast she had no chance to move out of his way. His arms closed around her, pinning her to him so that she couldn't breathe. She felt faint. She was going to die here, in this dark embrace. Claude's words came to her through a fog of panic.

"I need no devious methods to hold a woman in my arms," he said harshly. "I'm holding you now, and I'll hold you as long as I want to. No-one will interrupt us. I can do as I wish with you."

Tania looked into his dark, angry face. "Then do it," she mouthed at him. "Prove your brute strength if you must. You're holding me physically, but that's all. Emotionally, you don't even touch me. Are you capable of knowing the difference?"

There was total silence for a moment, and Tania prayed he would never know what it cost her to say what she did. Emotionally, her spirit cried out to him not to be like this. To be gentle, considerate, to want her for herself, not just because she was a woman in the usual sense of the word. She wanted to be his woman, *his*, exclusively, eternally, but she stared him out, her amber eyes darkened with fear and determination. If he had ever doubted that she had as much spirit as her brother James, even if it was channelled in different directions, he believed it now.

He let her go. She stood with her arms taut at her sides. She knew she had won in a battle of wills. Unbelievably, she had won. He could have taken her there and then. Proved his male superiority once and for all. She could see by the tightness of the muscles working in his neck and jaw that it had cost him a great effort of will not to do so. He wasn't used to being turned down. Still less to being faced with a young woman defying all his seduction, and telling him scornfully to get on with it if he must, because it wouldn't mean a thing to her.

Tania felt her whole body tremble. It would have meant the sun and stars, but not this way . . . not this way.

"I won't go immediately, Claude." She couldn't stop the huskiness in her voice. "I don't mean to leave you entirely in the lurch, and it would be best to let Henri realise gradually that I can't stay here for ever."

She held her breath, praying that he wouldn't demand to know why not. She was weary of battle. She couldn't begin all over again. He still said nothing, seating himself back at his desk.

"I'll stay another month," she went on. "I think that's a fair offer, don't you?"

"Two months instead of six?"

"I never promised to stay for six months. You know that." She wouldn't lose her temper again. "It's the best I can do. Take it or leave it. Only, please, if I stay, it must be strictly on a business basis from now on. Strictly, Claude."

"I see. I'm expected to agree to conditions as well now, am I? Do you make such impossible demands of your David Lee? And does he agree to them?" His tone said he couldn't believe any red-blooded man would be so emasculated.

"I don't need to," Tania said bluntly. "I'm comfortable with David. That's a word I can hardly apply to my relationship with you!"

"Comfortable!" Claude said explosively. "That's the last way I would want to describe my relationship with a woman! I can be comfortable with an old sofa or a favourite pair of slippers! God help me if I can't make a woman feel anything more than comfortable when I make love to her!"

She hadn't been talking about making love. It hadn't entered into her relationship with David, but she saw no reason to give him that little bit of ammunition against David.

"Do you agree or not?" Tania demanded to know. "One more month on my terms, or nothing."

Claude leaned back in his chair. He accepted too readily. His hands spread wide, as if in total capitulation.

"I agree! How can I do otherwise? But after all this trauma, I think we'll take the day off. I don't feel like working. I shall go and find some amusement elsewhere. The château is becoming a little inhibiting today. I'm sure you can find plenty to do. Go out with the others, or write to your David."

He taunted her, but she let it pass. She wouldn't think what his other amusements might be. She had seen some of them at the party, beautiful, olive-skinned girls who would probably be incredulous that she, a mere English girl, would refuse all that Claude Girard had to offer. She left the study abruptly, her head truly throbbing now. The tension of facing him after the late night was really getting to her, and instead of going out anywhere, Tania decided to have a lie-down for an hour. She would be bothering no-one, and she sought the serenity of her room as if it was a sanctuary.

One more month. One more month with Claude, and then she need never see him again. Her life would be as it was before. The slow, silent tears trickled down her cheeks and into her mouth as she lay with her eyes closed on her bed. She tasted them, salty, bitter, and knew that nothing would ever be the same for her, ever again. She knew the pain of love, and it seemed she was destined never to know the pleasures.

It was strange to be the only person having lunch at the château that day. The vast place seemed to echo with reproach, as if in protest against the English girl who dared to thwart its heir. Tania was waited on by the château servants, thinking foolishly she could just as easily have cooked up something for herself in Claude's kitchen. She would never dare to invade the main kitchens, but in Claude's quarters, she would have felt less conspicuous. The thing that stopped her was that he could very well have come back and found her there, and she had no wish to appear domesticated in his own kitchen. It took very little for him to see it as a submission.

She wouldn't write to David, Tania thought recklessly. She would phone him. Madame had been telling her for weeks to phone home whenever she wished, and she had done so on very few occasions. She would phone Lance too, and let him know that she wouldn't be staying over here for six months, regardless of what Claude Girard had told him! She wouldn't give a definite date. She was a little cautious. Maybe he'd try and persuade her that she should stay, since Claude was paying. Men had a strange habit of closing ranks, Tania had discovered. It was best to keep it vague, and just prepare the way.

At least David was overjoyed when she told him she wouldn't be staying in France until Christmas.

"Thank goodness for that, darling," he said enthusiastically. "Christmas wouldn't be the same without you. You'll come to us as usual this year, then, won't you? Mother will be pleased when I tell her."

She liked David's mother. Small, round and grey, complacently filling her days with an endless round of knitting for the four grandchildren, and obviously hoping that Tania would be the next addition to the family, to provide more work for Mrs Lee's perpetual-motion knitting needles. Tania couldn't repress a shiver as the inevitability of life with David was loosely translated to mean life with Mother as well . . .

"I expect so," Tania said brightly.

"I'll have to tell her, Tania. It's not fair to leave it until the last minute. You know she likes to plan well ahead. There are the puddings to make, and the cake— "

"For goodness' sake, it's only just September." She knew she sounded irritable and couldn't help it. She hated such long-term commitments on such trivial matters. The real, important things in life, like sharing two lives, were another matter. Christmas puddings could be bought at the supermarket at a minute's notice. She knew she was nit-picking with David, and that it wasn't his fault she alternated between ecstasy and despair, with the emphasis on the latter right now, she thought gloomily.

Suddenly realising there was a little silence at the other end of the line, and imagining so clearly David's look of surprised hurt at her snapping, Tania spoke more gently.

"David, it's very kind of your mother to invite me, and I promise I'll let you know in good time what my plans are," she hedged, hardly knowing why she did so.

"It's not just *kind*, darling. You know Mother sees you as practically one of the family already," David said boisterously.

Tania stared at the phone. He shouldn't have said *already*, her brain harped at her. As if there was never any doubt . . . Tania suddenly saw herself drawn into Mother Lee's cosy little afternoon tea meetings, and being urged to serve on Mother Lee's boring committees, like the dutiful wives of David's brothers. Sucked into a close-knit web of old-homestead living. The Lee wives didn't pursue careers. Their careers were in being wives and mothers, and more significantly, Lee daughters-in-law! David wouldn't exactly put pressure on her to resign from the company, but the pressure would be there just the same. From all sides, warm and smothering, like treacle.

"David, I'll have to go now," Tania said in quick short tones, because until this minute she had never seen things so clearly, nor questioned her future so dispassionately, and it alarmed her. Had she really been drifting along with the tide towards a marriage in which she wouldn't be merely David's wife, but also part of the Family, one of the buzzing little workers, the centre of which was the Queen Bee, Mother Lee!

She shook herself, wondering if she was going mad.

"All right, darling." David was as agreeable as ever.

How had she ever become involved with someone so luke-warm! The thought raced around in her head, and she hated herself for it, knowing that it was only by comparison . . .

"Hey," he said suddenly. "I miss you. Come home soon."

"Goodbye, David. I'll be in touch." She slammed down the phone. Her eyes smarted. She heard his words still ringing in her ears like afterthoughts, the little ritualistic finale to a telephone conversation. Usually he added a bit more. Love you. Miss you. See you soon.

Tania pushed the hair back from her forehead where it lay in heavy damp strands. The day was oddly oppressive after the glorious summer sunshine, and it was certainly taking its toll on her. What on earth was wrong with her? She was seeing shadows in every corner, picking up nuances in a voice that weren't really there. If she were the crying kind, she would have felt like weeping. It was all so illogical. If she examined her reasons for snubbing David, and Claude too, she could hardly make sense of them. A psycho-analyst would have a field-day with her. Here she was, nostalgic over the fact that she never had the type of family who gave her their time, their presence, and when it was offered to her on a plate, in the shape of the loving Lees, she rejected it with horror. Just what *did* she want?

The answer to that was too uncomfortable to think about, and she wouldn't let herself. There was no future for her with Claude Girard. Not unless he changed totally, gave up his lifestyle and the danger it contained . . . but then he wouldn't be the same man. Oh, damn him for getting under her skin the way he had, Tania thought angrily. It wasn't love. It was infatuation, a kind of repulsive attraction for someone who fascinated even while he threatened. There was enough psychological evidence for that kind of attraction! She wouldn't think of him any more.

123

By the time the rest of the Girards came back from their day out, Tania was feeling more relaxed. A long bath and a read on her bed had let the tangled tension unwind a little. A breeze had lifted some of the heavy still air, and she could laugh at some of her foolish fancies. She belonged to no-one. She could do whatever she wished, go where she liked. Instead of the fact dragging her down, it should uplift her, exhilarate her. She was no clinging vine, dependent on a man's whims. The book she read echoed the same sentiments, and by the time she dressed for dinner, Tania felt more able to listen to Henri's excited tales of Biarritz and the lovely day out they had had.

"You should have come with us, Tania," Monique smiled at her. "It was so good by the sea— "

"Denis came too," Henri interrupted. "He met us at the café, and Maman blushed to see him."

"Don't be silly, Henri," Monique laughed, but Tania saw that she was blushing now, her olive skin faintly pink.

"It was the unexpectedness of it," Madame put in, her eyes twinkling. "I told Denis he should surprise Monique more often."

Her meaning was clear. They all wanted Monique to marry again, and she and Denis seemed ideally suited, and were obviously in love. But Monique held back, probably because of Henri's handicap, refusing to name the day. Couldn't she see that it was the best thing for them all, and that Henri adored his future stepfather?

"Where is Claude?" Madame said in surprise. "Isn't he here?"

Tania flushed now. "He went out before lunch. I haven't seen him since, Madame."

Right on cue, Alphonse appeared in the room to say

that Monsieur Claude had just telephoned to say he was dining out with a friend, and wouldn't be back until late that evening.

Tania wondered just who the friend was, and knew it was no business of hers. Neither did she have the right to feel the burning stab of jealousy, when she had rejected every advance Claude made to her. He was a normal, healthy man. If she didn't want him, there were plenty of women who would. The sudden emptiness inside her made her almost dizzy. She had eaten too small a lunch, she thought determinedly. She needed food. Not for a single second would she admit that the hunger she felt was of a more basic, desperate kind.

There was no chance of hearing when Claude's car came back to the château late that night. Tania's room was at the rear of the building, and she would not be so foolish as to wait up, or lie rigidly awake in her bed, listening for the click of his light in the silence, or the soft pad of footsteps. Even through the thick château walls, the silence magnified small sounds, especially when someone's ears were specially attuned for them.

Whom had he been with until so late, she found herself thinking? Some beautiful, voluptuous woman who would give him all the comfort he needed? Some unknown woman who would have felt all the force of Claude Girard's undoubted masculinity, and sent him on his way with a reluctance and a sweet store of memories until the next time?

And she, fool that she was, Tania's thoughts whispered through her senses in that vulnerable hour of the night, could have known all this. It had been hers for the taking.

125

She tossed and turned, finding sleep elusive, impossible. Her throat was dry as sand. She must get a drink of water. The nearest place was Claude's kitchen. The château corridors were still maze-like to Tania, but she could easily go through his quarters to his kitchen.

She slid her feet into soft mules and pushed her arms through the sleeves of the Chinese silk robe. The whole château was wrapped in silence now. She closed her door very quietly, crept through the connecting door in the corridor to Claude's quarters, and by the dim light through the end window, made her way down the stairs to the kitchen. She drank a whole tumblerful of cold water, letting it trickle down her dry throat. Maybe after that she would get some sleep.

As she made her way back to her room, she suddenly heard sounds that made her heart stop for a minute, and then race on, the blood pounding in her ears. The sounds came from Claude's room. She stopped outside, listening. Even if the words were indistinct, the tortured mutterings were obvious. And then her heart leapt as she heard her brother's name.

"No, no, James, hold on . . . hold on. Oh God, no, dear God, help us somebody. Help us . . . James, James . . ."

He must be in the grip of some horrific nightmare, Tania thought. Still clinging to the precipice from where her brother had plunged to his death, reliving that terrible day. She hardly realised that her hand was clinging to the door handle, or that she was turning it. She hardly knew how it was that one minute she was standing outside the room, her heart seemingly clenched in as great a nightmare as Claude, and the next, she was inside, moving across to the bed where he writhed and swore furiously at the fates, bathed in gleaming sweat as he threshed about, no longer safe in bed at the Château Girard, but somewhere up there, in the mountains. Though he fought within himself with all the rage of a demented animal, Tania knew he held no fears for her at that moment.

She sped across his room to his bathroom, wrung out a face-cloth in cool water, and came to his bedside, to wipe away some of the salt sweat on his skin. In the blue cast of moonlight from the window, his features looked gaunt, ravaged, the eyes open and staring, yet not seeing her. Seeing nothing but the torment that was still inside him. And Tania felt a momentary fury at herself that she had never allowed herself to recognise it. She had seen only what she wanted to see.

Claude still babbled on, half-unintelligible, half so clear as to tear her heart apart. In their work they had not yet approached the fateful day when James had died. She had been dreading it, but never had she expected to be hearing it so graphically, so emotionally, so heartrendingly truthfully. Claude raged on in French, but she understood him perfectly, understanding the words and the man. He seemed unaware that she was there, despite the fact that when he went rigid with the shock of memory he clutched at her arms, or else she held him close to her, hearing his racing heartbeats. Or else she soothed him with whispered words, bathing his face, and his throat, and the broad expanse of his shoulders.

She still felt in no danger of him physically. He was someone in need of help, and she was giving it, hearing the rambling torment lessen a little, and the voice become quieter. Then, to her horror, his arms became vice-like around her, pulling her on to the bed with him. The stinging scent of his animal sweat didn't repulse her. A wild rippling of excitement held her. She hadn't asked to be here like this, nor to witness something of which Claude would be horrified in the morning, but she was here, and so was he, and his restlessness was calming, as if her presence was the only thing to restore his sanity. He still muttered wildly, but less aggressively, and now it was no longer James's name he spoke rapidly in his native tongue, but hers.

"If you go away, Tania, the sun will go out of my life. Having you here has been like the answer to a prayer. I need you like a flower needs rain. I'll go on having these nightmares for the rest of my life without you. You cannot be so cruel as to leave me. Swear that you will not. Swear it!"

His arms were so hard around her that she felt unable to breathe properly. Her breasts were crushed against his chest, their heartbeats vibrating like one person. He exerted every ounce of his will over her to get his way. He made no sexual advances, yet sensuality was in every pore of his skin, every movement he made or didn't make. Knowing him for the sensual man he was, she felt a fleeting admiration for the way he made no attempt to take physical advantage of the situation. Or was he being extraordinarily clever? Knowing that he was sending her mind into little spirals of desire, blinding her senses. She was becoming incapable of conscious thought. She could only feel, and want, and need. And all that she wanted was being denied her . . .

"What – what is it you want of me, Claude?" her mumbling voice was thickened. She could taste the salt of his skin as he pulled her face close to his, so that her mouth moved against his lips.

"I need you," he whispered back, skin touching skin,

moving seductively softly. Her dark hair fell against his face, and one of his hands captured a handful of it as if he would hold her there for ever. "I need you to belong to me, now and for ever. Do you know what I'm saying, Tania? Not for an hour or a day, but for ever. I want to know that you're mine."

The words penetrated into her mind like little darts of quivering pleasure. She had never known this intensity of passion, of desire, of need before. Her blood surged with a matching need. His voice drugged her, demanding total submission. His free hand moved slowly downwards over the Chinese silk, down her back to the slender curve of her waist and over her rounded buttocks, to remain still for a moment before returning up the length of her body to tighten possessively again. She was holding her breath, unsure whether to be glad or ragingly frustrated, admitting to both.

"Tell me you won't leave me, *chérie*." His voice became more aggressive as she didn't, couldn't answer. "I may as well have died on the mountain with James if you go. Tell me you couldn't be so heartless. You belong to me. You belong here. We both know it. You will stay here and be my wife, and there will be no talk of going back to your sterile work and your pathetic David. You and I will reach the top of the mountains together, my Tania."

"I – I— " she felt as if she were drowning, not sure if she had heard him properly. Or had she merely dreamed that he was asking her to be his wife? And if he was, then was this what she wanted? Was this after all her destiny, to live in danger's shadow yet again? The wild refusal trembled on her tongue, as the inherent fear rushed back at her with the speed of lightning.

And then Claude's mouth was claiming hers in a long

sweet beautiful kiss, his hands cupping her face, no longer fierce and demanding, leaving her body free to escape, to run, to go as far away as she could, to forget this night had ever happened. To forget to breathe . . .

He moved his mouth away from hers, his soft breath still warming her. And she knew that she was still held by him, held by the devil-magic of his touch and his need, and held by her own femininity that reached out to him as surely as night followed day. She was helpless against such power.

"Marry me, Tania. Be my wife. Be my love."

"Yes, yes, oh yes," she heard herself say with a little sigh against his lips, for it was so sweet not to fight him any longer, and to say what her heart dictated at last.

Chapter 8

Tania awoke with the nagging feeling that something was wrong. She glanced at her bedside clock, registering with a shock that it was past ten o'clock and she must have slept right through her alarm, struggling out of bed, before she remembered. It was the surprise of seeing she was wearing her Chinese robe in bed that brought every tingling moment back to her, and hot colour flooded through her whole body.

She had come back here, utterly drained, to fall into bed and to sleep immediately. Ironic, when she had had such difficulty before. But it was where she had been, and what had happened, that scalded into her mind right now. Claude had had a nightmare, and she had gone to him, soothed him, and somehow, somehow she had said she would *marry* him . . . Her heart beat so loudly she felt as if it would burst.

He couldn't have meant it when he proposed to her. He wasn't the marrying kind. James had said so. She had seen it for herself. He had humiliated her, and this morning he would mock her for her stupid gullibility in believing it. Maybe he had even manufactured the nightmare just to stage all this . . . no, that had been real. Tania would stake her life on that.

But all the rest . . . she closed her eyes in mortification.

How could she have been so gullible? And how was she going to face him this morning? Working together, knowing that he knew she could be tempted after all. How was she going to spend the last few weeks working with him in such an atmosphere?

She couldn't, of course. In humiliating her as he had done, he must be made to see that he had forfeited the right to her presence here. She would tell him after breakfast, and then she would leave. She would go home. The word had a hollow sound to it, for this lovely place had been more of a home to her in these last weeks than any other she had ever known.

She showered and dressed quickly, wondering why no-one had come to waken her. She hurried down to the dining-room, to find with a little shock that Claude and his mother were still there, lingering over coffee. Henri would be preparing for his tutor's arrival, and Monique had gone to the boutique. When Tania appeared, Claude got up at once, came to the door to meet her, and pulled her into his arms. She was too surprised to move away, and then, unbelievably, she heard Claude's voice, tender, caring, as he spoke to her.

"Good morning, *chérie*. I thought you'd like a lie-in after our long discussion last night. I've told Mother our wonderful news, and Monique is bringing some gowns home for your approval this afternoon."

Tania gaped at him, but before she could say anything, Madame had got up, to kiss her lightly on the cheeks, a delighted smile on her face.

"Tania, *chérie*, I could not be more pleased. You will be a beautiful bride, and so very welcome into our family."

"Thank you, Madame," she stammered, frustrated at

the way Claude had obviously told his mother the news already. How dare he . . . and yet, what was more natural? Or did he suspect that by now she would have had second thoughts, seen sense, realised how impossible it was to marry him? She couldn't marry him! Not without betraying her own feelings, and she was quite sure they weren't reciprocated on Claude's side. He needed her for his own ego, because he wasn't used to women rejecting him. Only in Tania's case, he'd had to go farther than ever before. He'd offered marriage. Even if she went through with it because of her own weakness in loving him, how long would it be before he became bitter towards her? Feeling that she had forced him into a marriage he didn't really want?

Was she crazy, thinking like that? *He* was forcing *her*, not the other way around! She took a deep breath, ignoring the way Claude's fingers were digging into her arms. She wished desperately that his closeness didn't affect her so much. Whether he was aggressive or tender, he could still send the tremor through her veins.

"I was about to say that I think I should go back to England very soon," she dared him to try anything on in front of his mother when, to her astonishment, he nodded approvingly.

"I was saying the very same to Mother. We will go tomorrow, *chérie*. You will be able to collect anything you want from your flat and give in your notice there, and also at your work. Then we will personally visit as many friends as you wish to invite to the wedding, and all expenses will be met by me, of course. You will want to have some of your English friends at the ceremony."

"It has been a long time since we had a wedding at the château, Tania." Her eyes turned, trance-like to Madame

Girard, as Claude's mother went on enthusiastically. "Monique's was the last time, to Henri's father, and it was so beautiful. You will make a very lovely bride, Tania, and I'm sure you will love the selection of clothes Monique will bring this afternoon."

"Clothes?" she said faintly, feeling as if none of this was happening, that she couldn't be so feeble as to be taken over completely like this. Madame still smiled, sensing nothing of Tania's confusion, and obviously assuming the girl to be a little distracted at her sudden engagement. What girl wouldn't?

"For your trousseau, my dear," Madame went on patiently. "And your wedding-gown, naturally. Monique thought you would prefer to try them all on in your room here, but if you want to change your mind, I'm sure Claude will drive you into Toulouse instead."

"Oh no. Here will be fine," Tania said through dry lips. A trousseau. Wedding-gown. The sweet images blurred. Claude was determined to go through with it, then, and she was doing nothing to stop it. She should scream and rage that all this had come about because of a cheap trick on Claude's part. A seduction of her senses . . . but somehow she remained dumb, knowing it was more than she could do after all, to resist what life was offering her. For once she would go towards it fearlessly, without stopping to think of tomorrow, of that chain of communication centred in Claude's office that would call him from her side when the snows came, she *wouldn't* think of it.

"I've told Mother we'll have to give your English friends a little time to get used to the idea of our marriage, and to make their arrangements. We can accommodate them here, of course. But we can tell them all that when we go to England tomorrow." Claude was very smooth. "We will have plenty to do to make all the arrangements for two weeks' time, won't we?"

Tania felt her heart leap. He was rushing her, giving her no time to think.

"We can't possibly be ready in two weeks." Her voice seemed to squeak in her ears, but evidently it didn't, because no-one seemed to notice.

Madame laughed gently. "Tania, we can do anything we set our minds to if we try!" she said, with the assurance of one who had only to ask and it would be done. "Don't worry, *chérie*, your wedding will take place in two weeks' time, and you will be serene and beautiful. Just concentrate on being happy, both of you, and leave the organising to others."

She didn't dare look at Claude. Was he happy? Was she? She didn't feel in the least the way a bride should feel, except for the jitters inside. At least those were real. She didn't know how she felt, least of all how Claude viewed this marriage. In a sudden flurry of uncertainty, she prayed he hadn't expected her to sue him for breach of promise or something equally nasty.

When they were alone in his study, she faced him, her hands clenched at her sides. She had to know.

"Claude, I didn't expect you to have told your mother and sister about – about— "

"Our marriage, Tania. Are you afraid to say the word?" he said deliberately, and she flushed.

"Last night— " she began haltingly, feeling acutely embarrassed at the way she had gone to him, and seen him at his most vulnerable. Claude, strong and powerful, would hate anyone to know he suffered from the most human of nightmares.

"Last night need have been a secret known only to the two of us if you had wished it," she said steadily. "I would never have held you to anything you said, Claude. I want you to know that, and if you want to change your mind, it's not too late."

"It's very generous of you to say you'd never hold me to my proposal," he said curtly. "The fact remains that I have every intention of holding you to your acceptance. I asked you to be my wife and you said you would. The date is fixed, and I have already made some phone calls to the priest and the florist and made a honeymoon reservation. Now, do you want to do some work this morning, or will your head be too full of other things to concentrate?"

Her mouth had dropped open. Was this her future husband, this, cold, hard man who spoke of honeymoon plans as if he referred to a business meeting? If she had not known that he could be so very different from the way he appeared right now, she might have told him to get lost, and she would never have married him if he was the last man on earth. As it was, Tania swallowed, said meekly that she would rather work, and bent her head over her pad as she sat down abruptly, so that he wouldn't see the bewildering mixture of emotions in her eyes.

Things moved so quickly after that, Tania was left almost gasping. This was the way things happened when you had money and influence, she thought faintly. The gowns Monique brought to the château were so lovely, she wanted them all, and was foolish enough to say so in front of Madame, who insisted that she should. There was exquisite lingerie and nightgowns, and three fabulous wedding-gowns and accessories from which to choose. Monique had unerring taste when it came to knowing exactly what Tania would want, and which suited her best, and she chose a flowing lace creation, with floor-length veil, held at the sides of the head with tiny pearl-centred flowers. Tania moved about as if she was in a dream . . . would she wake up soon and find it was all a cruel mirage, that instead of everything she had nothing?

Next day she and Claude flew to London. She had made a list of the people she would want at her wedding, including David, though she knew instinctively that he wouldn't come. She could hardly blame him, but she insisted on seeing him on her own and breaking the news. He looked shattered, but Tania knew him well enough to suspect that his emotions didn't run as deeply as other people's. He would soon get over it.

Lance Hillman was amazed and delighted, though sorry to be losing her services in the company. She was an excellent linguist, he told Claude, clearly still a little stunned that Tania should be marrying him, knowing all her earlier feelings towards him.

"I'm sure she'll be an excellent wife," Claude smiled back at Lance. "And you'll agree that my need is greater than yours."

"I'm quite sure it is," Lance laughed, reassured. "I should hope so, anyway. And thank you for the invitation. Josie and I will be delighted to come. You're sure you want the kids too?"

"I must have some family around me," Tania said quickly. "Even if it's only an adopted one. I've asked a couple of the girls in my department as well, and I know you'll all love the château. It's very beautiful."

"That's what she's marrying me for, you know," Claude said lightly, his eyes teasing. At Lance's sudden worried glance, Tania threaded her arm in Claude's, leaned towards his face, and pressed her soft lips to his. It was a gesture for Lance's benefit, but however trite the meaning, her mouth still tingled from the contact with Claude's, and she was aware of the slight indrawing of his breath.

"Don't let him fool you, Lance," she said, her voice breathy. "He knows I love him as much as he loves me."

The poignancy of her words left her thick in the throat, but it obviously relieved Lance to hear them. Claude didn't love her, he only desired her, and he was prepared to go to these lengths to possess her. She must be stark raving mad to ever have agreed to it, but she was learning fast that she was powerless to stop it now. She simply didn't have the strength of will to deny herself a few brief weeks of happiness . . . because she was sure it wouldn't last. It couldn't. Their personalities would clash all too soon, especially when winter came, and the mountains called to Claude. For the time being there was no question of his doing sponsored climbs.

The limp in his leg was barely noticeable, but there was still a weakness there that would make such climbs foolhardy. He had told her as much, in a clipped, angry voice that said how much he resented having his stamina questioned. But in any mountain rescue attempt, if other men's lives were in danger, Tania knew instinctively that if Claude was in the vicinity, he would be alongside his team. And she would be the woman waiting for news.

They stayed at an hotel in London for one night, and Tania was glad that Claude had booked separate rooms. As if he had no need to force the issue now. In two weeks he could have his fill of her, and the thought was both spine-tingling and unnerving. She was marrying a stranger, yet he had never been a stranger to her.

The first night of their meeting, when he had come to her flat, there had been a spark of instant recognition that went far beyond the mere fact that she had seen his face in magazines, and heard about him from James. There had been the kind of recognition that transcended human awareness; a reaching out of mind and thought as if from somewhere in a distant past; an inherited memory of sharing some other lifetime of love in another existence.

Tania asked herself shakily if she was becoming deranged by this man. Her spheres of consciousness seemed more sharply defined, as if all her senses were capable of embracing facets of awareness hitherto unknown to her. As if, with him at her side, she was truly capable of conquering mountains.

Two weeks later, she was asking herself if those thoughts had ever been hers. Facing herself in the long mirror of her bedroom in the Château Girard, an unreal vision stared back at her, a vision seemingly incapable of coherent thoughts, let along such introspective ones. The beautiful white lace wedding-gown softly emphasised her rounded shape without being unduly seductive. The cloud of veiling caressed her, the pearls and flowers at her cheeks softening the stark beauty of her face. Her hair was drawn back to allow the bridal attire to have the full effect, and it lay, glossy and full, on her shoulders. To Tania's own eyes, she was pale, her skin needing a touch of colour on her cheeks. Her mouth was a soft pale pink, and only her eyes seemed to shine with an ambre lustre that was brilliant to anyone else; startlingly afraid to her own gaze. Inside, she was numb. She couldn't think what she was doing here, in this charade, the principal character.

Downstairs, in this beautiful setting, flowers adorned the main stairway and hall of the château. Flowers were everywhere. Their perfume filled the air, heady and strong. On the bed lay Claude's bridal bouquet. Pink budding roses, laced with stephanotis and fern, fragrant, reminding her of summer, even though summer was over. How soon would this farce of a marriage be over? Tania thought chokingly.

"Oh, you are so beautiful, Tania," Monique's soft voice spoke behind her, and Tania turned quickly, the mask of happiness back on her face. Downstairs, friends and relatives waited for her. The strains of music were already evident from below. Henri was dressed in a velvet suit in his wheel-chair, solemnly awaiting her appearance. Claude was waiting also.

"I'm ready," she whispered, picking up the bouquet.

Monique hugged her quickly, telling her to be happy, and the two of them went down the stairs. At the last minute, Tania had thought to ask Lance to give her away, and he stood proudly at the foot of the wide curving staircase, his arm ready for her. Without it, Tania felt as if she would have fainted.

And then there was no more time to be afraid, because the music grew stronger, and the guests rose to their feet, and Lance was taking her to where Claude stood waiting for her, dark and handsome, waiting to say the words that would bind him to her and she to him. And once she reached him, Tania became oddly calm, all fears forgotten, repeating the vows in French, in a low, positive voice, and hearing Claude do the same. Finally, the heavy gold rings exchanged, he lifted the veil from her face, looked deeply into her eyes for a long penetrating moment, and then folded her to his chest, kissing her for the first time as man and wife.

Claude's wife . . . everything after that was a blur as far as Tania was concerned. Everything was a mere marking of time until the wedding feast was over, the champagne drunk, the two of them had changed out of their wedding finery into travelling clothes, and they were being driven off in a limousine to the airport at Bordeaux. Claude hadn't told her where they were going, and she felt absurdly shy about asking him. This was her honeymoon, and she couldn't ask her bridegroom the simple question of where she would spend her wedding night!

She glanced at his face in the back of the limousine beside her. Alphonse drove swiftly and smoothly, and Claude seemed to be miles away. She had never felt less like a bride! She prayed that it wasn't going to be a complete disaster, for both their sakes. As if he sensed her watching him, he turned to her, and she felt his fingers reach out to curl around hers in the back of the car. The contact gave her a small feeling of warmth. He leaned across, brushing her cheek with his lips, like any bridegroom. Not every bridegroom would have uttered his words though.

"Don't worry. I won't eat you. At least, not all at once."

Tania got the extraordinary feeling that he was a bit nervous too, and the thought was so ludicrous she could have laughed out loud. But the tension was lessened a little, and at last she felt able to ask where they were going.

"Are you always this impatient, my lovely bride?" A smile played around his mouth. Alphonse couldn't hear what they said, since the glass screen was between the front and back of the limousine, but they must have appeared a loving couple at that moment, whispering sweet nothings to each other.

"I'd just like to know," she retorted, not wanting any double meanings to come into his words.

"Paris," he stated, and Tania's eyes widened with delight. It could have been anywhere, one of the Greek islands in total isolation, or farther afield, but she had always loved Paris, and hadn't been back there since her schooldays.

"I thought you'd like it," he went on. "The weather isn't at its best now, but we can play at being tourists, see some shows, and make new memories to add to all your old ones of the city. It's also bustling enough that we don't need to be alone every minute. I gather that suits you, Madame Girard?"

The name made her start, but of course it was hers now. His astute comment made her cheeks tinge with colour too. She longed to be alone with him, and yet she dreaded it. She had every right in the world, and yet she had no rights. She had no idea why he thought she had married him. Maybe it was because he really did think she fancied herself as mistress of the château. What he never suspected was the true reason, that she loved him. She loved him so much, and to Tania's mind, that meant she had married him under false pretences.

Reasons, excuses, motives, all of them faded away when they finally reached the lovely hotel overlooking the lovely River Seine, its bridges mellow in the evening lights from the city. Paris was beautiful in the daytime, but simply sparkled at night, like a beautiful woman dressed up to show off to her admirers. She glittered, she glowed, she enticed, and Claude's pleasure in Tania's excited delight at being here made the two of them behave almost naturally in this artificial environment.

In the honeymoon suite of the hotel, he had ordered pink roses to adorn every room. It was a mad extravagance, but when Tania giggled slightly over it, he told her gravely that it should remind her of the first time he had proposed to her.

"The first time?" She was brought up short from her exploration of the lovely rooms. They had drunk a bottle of champagne placed to chill in their bedroom, and Tania had discovered that there was more in a small fridge in the main salon. "What first time? I only remember you saying it once!"

And how easily she had said yes, how quickly he had taken command when she did so, and now they were here, like this . . . Tania felt a shiver of nervous excitement run through her.

"Have you forgotten so soon, that day on the patio at the château when you were surrounded by pink rose petals that were dropping at your feet?" Claude smiled at her.

Yes, she had forgotten. She had forgotten how he had come creeping up on her conversation with his mother, and said there was another way to get her to remain in France, and that was to marry him. Of course she had forgotten. It wasn't meant to be taken seriously . . . was it?

"Are we going downstairs for dinner?" she said, suddenly nervous. He smiled slowly, lazily, the predator with no need to hurry, because his kill was his for the taking. Her heart throbbed loudly.

"No. Dinner is coming to us," he said, and within minutes there was a tap on the door and a laden trolley was pushed into the room by a discreet waiter. Claude told him not to come back for the trolley, and that they had everything they needed. Her face burned, reading the implications of that remark.

She hardly noticed what they ate, though it was a superbly cooked meal. She was too conscious of the mounting tension between them, vibrant and electric. Each time Claude's fingertips touched her, she felt a little shock, at once pleasurable and unbearably emotional. When they had drained the coffee pot, he looked across the table at her. The time for pretending was over. She could read it in his dark, demanding eyes.

"I – I think I'll take a shower," she stammered, suddenly nervous.

"Yes, do. And then it will be time for bed." At her small flicker of alarm she couldn't quite hide, he reached out and grasped her hand, turning it over to kiss her palm. "Tania – you didn't expect this to be a marriage in name only, did you?"

"No," she whispered. "Of course not."

He let go of her hand. She almost fled to the bathroom, feeling all kinds of an idiot. She had never been so nervous in her life. Nor so angry with herself for showing it. She stripped off her clothes with trembling hands and stepped into the shower, letting the soft warm water cool her burning skin. She closed her eyes for a brief moment. The next instant they flew open again as the shower curtain was pulled aside, and she was briefly aware of Claude's naked body before he was stepping in beside her, closing the plastic curtain behind them, enclosing them in a private world of steam and perfumed sensuality.

"Get out of here— " she stuttered, and he laughed softly, picking up a bar of soap and rubbing it between his palms until it lathered up into a mass of foam.

"Don't be silly, Tania. You're my wife. For God's sake, relax. You're as tense as a spring. I won't hurt you. I'd never hurt you. Relax, *chérie*."

As he spoke he began to soap her body, spiralling over her breasts in gentle movements, so erotic that she was holding her breath as the nipples hardened in response. She was drowning in pleasure as the movements continued over her body, learning, exploring, seeking, always gentle, always seductively slow. She was in a silky, pampered world, with Claude's fingers holding the key to her happiness; she was intoxicated with the feelings he awoke in her.

"Your turn." His voice was seductive in her ear, and she felt the bar of soap pushed into her hands. Her face flamed. She couldn't! His dark, passion-dilated eyes bored into hers, insisting that she could. Like a robot, Tania lathered up the soap, and anything but robot-like, she began soaping Claude's body, feeling the maleness of his shape, the hair-roughened chest, the different texture of his skin. His eyes demanded everything of her, interspersed with little ghost kisses on her lips, her throat, her breasts . . . if she died tomorrow, Tania thought with mounting poignancy, at least she would have this – this knowledge of Claude's desire for her. This undeniable male need of her that was turning her knees to water, and causing her to tremble.

He turned off the shower, reaching through the curtain for a large bath towel. He patted her semi-dry, and then himself, and, their hair still dripping, he carried her out of the bathroom towards the huge bed. At some time he had turned off the main light, and the room was lit only by the glow of one table lamp. His eyes were gleaming like dark coals, and a thrill of heat ran through Tania's body. She ached, yearned for the fulfilment he promised her, and yet the anxiety pervading her body was a secret known only to herself, that was soon to be shared with another person.

"I wish I had the talent to paint you like this," Claude's hypnotic voice said in her ear. "With that soft pink glow on your beautiful body, you would put every goddess to shame. My beautiful bride – have you any idea how long I have waited for this, for you?"

He began to speak disjointedly, as if he too was overcome by something more inexplicable than the occasion, emotional though it was. His voice was urgent, too quick, so that she couldn't always hear it properly. Understandably so, since his mouth was making a journey of her satiny skin, as if he would learn its every contour by heart and touch, and her breathing was becoming more ragged by the minute, her heart racing.

She clung to his powerful shoulders as his body blotted out the lamplight, as his urgently whispered words that he could wait no longer, that he needed her so badly, so much, filled her head and her mind. This was Claude, whom she loved, and needed, for whom she would give the earth . . . She heard her own sharp cry of pain as the piercing sweetness drove past her suddenly mumbling words, but by then it was too late . . .

"Dear God, why didn't you tell me?" Claude's voice was an angry throb of pain adding to all the rest. "Why did you let me go on believing you were experienced? That you and that soupy David Lee had been lovers?"

"But I didn't," Tania said, the weak tears trickling down her face and into her neck. "What did you expect me to do – announce to the world that I'm still a virgin? At my age?"

Her hurt, mental and physical, showed in her brittle voice. Once he realised, Claude hadn't prolonged his lovemaking, but she felt doubly humiliated at the way he lay alongside her, clearly angry with himself and with her.

"Not to the world, just to me," he stated. "And you shouldn't feel shame, for Pete's sake! It's a rare and beautiful thing for a man to marry a virgin these days – but you should have warned me. I would have taken things more slowly."

Far from reassuring her, his remarks seemed to Tania to underline his own experience with women. He would have known what to do if she had told him, she thought bitterly. It didn't help her self-confidence one little bit to know it.

"I'm sorry I misled you," she said bitterly. "This whole thing has been a mistake, hasn't it? You couldn't get me into bed with you any other way, so you married me, and now you're probably wishing you hadn't bothered. I don't blame you. I'm wishing the same. Why did I ever let myself be talked into this! I could be home in England now, instead of living a lie with a man I hate!"

The words were out before she could stop them, all the old anger and misery, combined with her own self-condemnation. She should have had more sense, more self-control, than to let her heart rule her head. Look where it had led her! A furious Claude was looking down at her unbelievingly, and it was almost impossible to remember that those ice-cold eyes had once been devouring her with passion.

"You're quite a little actress, aren't you, my lovely wife?" Claude ground out. "So maybe I was right in my joking remark to your boss. Maybe you did marry me for the château after all!"

It was ludicrous. She would never do that, but she recognised his need to hurt her as she had hurt him, and she clamped her lips together rather than hurl any more insults at him. Claude took her silence as an admission of guilt, and flung himself out of the bed to pour himself some whisky from the salon fridge before he returned to the bedroom. Tania lay there, quaking with fright, knowing she had angered as well as humiliated him. Finally he spoke in a cold voice as he snapped out the lamplight, plunging the room into darkness. She felt the bed dip as he got in beside her, not touching her.

"Very well, Tania. You've got what you want, but equally, I shall have what I want. I want my wife, and we'll have no half-hearted arrangements. Do you understand me?"

"Yes," she said faintly. He meant that he still desired her, still meant to make love to her whenever he chose. In return she was mistress of the château, or at least, she would be when his mother died. It was what he believed she wanted. Tania closed her eyes, knowing he couldn't be more wrong. She would love him in a tent . . . A small sob broke from her lips, and she heard his sardonic voice, throbbing with leashed anger.

"Don't be alarmed, my sweet, I've no wish for a repeat performance tonight. I'll spare you that, since my lovemaking is clearly so abhorrent to you. But this is only a temporary respite, I promise you that."

He turned his back on her, and Tania lay there in the darkness, wondering bitterly if this could really be her wedding-night.

Chapter 9

Tania had scoffed at the cynical remark that a honeymoon could be a nightmare, but she wasn't scoffing now. The two weeks in Paris were a bigger strain on her nerves than anything she had ever experienced. She knew better than to suggest to Claude that they went home early. It would be losing face to him for anyone to suspect that the newlyweds weren't idyllically happy. He had made it clear on the morning after their disastrous wedding-night that the marriage was to continue, no matter what their feelings towards each other. There was no divorce in the Girard family.

Tania listened mutely. Her feelings hadn't changed, nor ever would. She lay there, in the beautiful white silk nightgown that was part of her trousseau, listening to the harsh words of her husband, and wondered how this had ever happened. Claude leaned up on one elbow, his bare bronze torso lit by splinters of sunlight through the window. He looked down at her, her chestnut hair fanned across the pillow, her amber eyes wide, mouth softened by sleep, and his own tightened.

"I want children, Tania," he spoke roughly. "I waited a long time before choosing the right wife for me, and I don't take easily to admitting I made a mistake."

She felt a sudden anger. "Yes, it was a mistake, wasn't

it! And I made one too. A ghastly, hideous mistake in thinking I could trust you! That night at the château, when you were in the throes of the nightmare – was that all put on for my benefit? So that you could catch me at a vulnerable moment and make your outrageous proposal? Do you think I would ever have accepted you at any normal, rational time?"

She gasped as he gripped her arms and pulled her from the pillow into his arms. His face was white, his eyes dark by contrast. She felt the power in his fingertips, in every part of him. She had hurled the words at him in fury, knowing all the time that his nightmare had been real, just as hers was now.

"I won't even answer that. Facts remain facts, and the most important one now is that you're my wife, and you will remain so. I apologise for the way I hurt you last night, but you must know that there are different degrees of making love. Passion can be shown in different ways, both tender and violent. Before we leave Paris, you will learn every one of them."

Tania was aware that his fingers had lessened their pressure, and were trailing softly up and down her bare arms. She shivered as a wave of yearning, of shuddering excitement, began its insidious invasion of her body. No matter that he had hurt her and insulted her by his arrogant male domination. Nothing mattered, but the inescapable fact. She was his wife, and though she had her own opinions on just how long she could live with him, knowing that he only wanted her to provide Girard children and continue the dynasty, she was totally unable to resist as she felt the cool white silk being tossed aside, and the warmth of Claude's body take its place next to her skin.

And now, in the pale light of morning, Claude set out to show her just how pleasurable love could be. Their limbs entwined, mouths touching, each a part of the other, two halves of one perfect being. Gone was the vigorous lover of last night, and in its place was a more gentle passion, that was none the less capable of taking her to the heights, to a place where she had never been until now. There was no thought of fear, no holding back.

The sensations she felt were nothing short of spectacular. At the same time, she felt oddly weightless, as if she was truly suspended in space and time for strange, long moments. It was almost as though there was a momentary loss of reason and self, as if she was no longer Tania Paget Girard, but truly a part of Claude. She had never felt this sense of belonging to another person in her life before, and it was an awesome feeling.

Slowly, very slowly, as if reluctant to break the spell, she lifted her eyelids. Above her, against the light, his dark head surrounded by a halo of sunlight, Claude's face was expressionless. Tania breathed in shallow gasps. Surely now he would tell her he loved her – that he wanted and desired her was indisputable. But she needed more, craved more. She needed the reassurance of love as well as the physical act.

He bent to kiss her softly parted mouth. She realised her fingernails were digging little crescents in his shoulders and slackened them a little. She gazed wordlessly into his face.

"Thank you," Claude said. Tania's eyelids flickered, tears pricking behind them.

"Thank you?" she whispered, completely stunned by such a comment, and too hurt to be angry, for surely such a shared, beautiful experience was not to be cheapened by thanks.

"For proving that there's a real, living, warm woman behind the façade," he said. He moved away from her in one sinuous movement, walking in unashamed nakedness to the bathroom. Her eyes watched him go. It was as if he took her very soul with him. She was drained, suddenly empty of feeling, and more alone than she had ever been in her life before.

It seemed that Claude was determined that they should enjoy Paris and take home with them a store of memories. They did all the tourist things, the museums and galleries and churches. They took a *bateau mouche* on the Seine, and saw Montmartre by moonlight. They marvelled at Versailles. They gorged themselves on good food and wine, and every night Claude made love to her. Made love . . . Were two words ever more inappropriately phrased, she thought poignantly?

It was never a mere mechanical act, for Claude was far too physical a man for that, and it seemed as if he deliberately set out to be as sensual as he could. With what motive, Tania couldn't be sure. Unless he hoped for her final surrender to him. Physically, he had it totally, but she was somehow just able to hold on to her senses enough so that she never betrayed herself. She never once said that she loved him. She could say "I love you" in more than half a dozen languages, but they were never spoken to her husband, and he never said them to her.

Why did he marry her? she thought desperately, as the days passed. Just to provide heirs to the Girard estate? Why *her*? Or was it some cruel sort of penance for James's death? A recompense . . . her heart filled with pain at the thought, but if she persisted in looking for reasons, it was one that she hated, and one that had never occurred to her until now. She wished very much that it hadn't.

"Have you enjoyed Paris?" Claude said quietly on the flight back. "I hope so, Tania."

"Yes, thank you. I've always loved Paris." They made trite, stilted small-talk. They were as unlike two people in love as it was possible to be. Naturally, Tania thought bitterly, because they were not two people in love. One of them was in love . . . and that was the worst pain of all.

"Claude, you said there was no divorce in the Girard family." The words were tumbling out before she could stop them. "And I'll stay as long as you need me for the book. But after that – surely you can see how impossible it is for us to go on like this? It's all a sham. As soon as it's convenient, I shall go back to England and you'll be free of me."

She stared straight ahead, at the back of the seat in front of her. He could think what he liked. If he didn't divorce her then they must stay separated until she could divorce him. It was unthinkable that they should continue married when he didn't love her. What a blind fool she had been to be swept off her feet by him in the first place. She should have listened to her instincts instead of her heart.

"No, you will not leave, Tania." She jumped as he spoke, his voice vibrating with anger. "No woman walks out on her marriage in my family."

"Women are liberated now, or haven't you heard?" she said with heavy sarcasm. "A wedding-ring doesn't shackle me for ever."

He forced her to look at him. His hand grasped her chin, twisting her face to meet his furious eyes. He bruised her.

"Is this what your so-called liberation does for you then? Makes a mockery of the vows made before God? Did it really mean nothing at all to you?"

Oh, please don't, her eyes begged him silently, *don't tear me apart like this.* She felt suddenly older and wiser than he, if he thought that words said before a priest were all that mattered. God knew the very heart of a man. A priest didn't. Any two people could stand before him and vow to love, honour and cherish, and mean nothing at all. A small sob was wrenched from her throat, and Claude let go of her at once. She put her hands feelingly to her jaw where he had held her.

Sunlight glinted on the heavy gold of her wedding-ring. Claude pulled her hand away from her face and caressed the cold metal on her suddenly lifeless finger.

"With this ring, I thee wed," he repeated in a low, deep voice. "And I keep what is mine."

He let her go, his resonant voice still drumming in her ears for the rest of the flight. Tania twisted away from him as far as she could. He was impossible. He acted like a cave-man. Why didn't he just drag her along by her hair and be done with it? she fumed inwardly, and there was no way she was going to remain at the château with him for a moment longer than necessary. She would leave, once she had fulfilled her promise with the book . . . though, remembering the utter isolation of the château, and its inaccessibility except by car, she felt a sudden qualm.

Then she told herself not to be so feeble. Maybe Alphonse would be informed not to take the young Madame anywhere with a suitcase, but there were other ways. She could phone for a taxi when the time came. She wouldn't be beaten.

It was a short flight from Paris to Bordeaux, and the

Girard limousine was there to meet them, with the implacable Alphonse at the wheel. No, Tania thought, there would be no help from such a staunch family retainer. It was best to go alone, and keep silent about her plans until she was ready.

In the speeding car as it covered the miles to the château, the countryside blurred to Tania. She was very tired, as much from mental exhaustion as anything else. These last two weeks . . . her honeymoon . . . yet they hadn't been all bad, or meaningless. Much of the time was unforgettable, and there had been times when she could pretend this barrier between her and Claude didn't really exist. There had been laughing, happy times, when they shared the joy of Paris and the exhilaration of being alive in a city made for lovers. There had been times when they had been those lovers, lost in each others' arms, learning the wonder of love, before the calculating mask came over Claude's face once more, and he turned away from her.

Did he begin to wonder how soon it would be before she conceived the child he wanted, Tania thought? Was that his sole concern? She hadn't suspected him of being so fiercely traditional, of wanting a son so keenly, or was it just a matter of pride, to prove that the Girard seed was vigorous and strong, and capable of producing an heir as quickly as possible? Or was it just to keep her here?

Tania dozed fitfully in the car, her head gradually dropping against Claude's shoulder. It felt safe there. There had been other times when she had felt safe, times he didn't know about. Sometimes she had woken in the night in the Paris hotel, and just lay there, listening to him breathing. She had run her fingers across his broad back and pressed her lips to it, tasting his skin, knowing that no-one could take this from her. Asleep, she could love him freely, openly, she could gain all the comfort she needed from his warmth, for only then was he the vulnerable one. If he lay on his back, she had kissed his mouth very gently, so as not to awaken him. She had breathed him, loved him, salted his face with her tears . . .

"We're home," Claude said. Tania moved her head away from his shoulder, wondering if she had still been dreaming, or if the butterfly kiss she had felt touch her mouth had been real at that moment. It was too dark to tell. Ahead of them, the château was a blaze of lights, and Tania felt a frisson of relief that other people would be inside, to lessen the tension between her and Claude. It was a sad thought to take home with her after a honeymoon.

They sensed the air of cautious excitement at once. Madame Girard, whom she must now call Mother if she could manage it, she had been informed, came to greet Tania with a kiss, before she turned to Claude. When she asked if they had enjoyed themselves, the awkward question was relieved by Monique's laughing rejoinder that she shouldn't ask such personal questions, and they only had to look at the newlyweds to know that they were happy.

Tania was amazed at the remark. Or did everyone naturally assume that because newlyweds were expected to be happy, then they *were* happy? Maybe no-one looked beyond the expectation. If that was the case, Tania was fervently glad of it, to save any embarrassment. For a wild moment, she wondered what the reaction would be if she suddenly yelled out that it had been an appalling two weeks, and that all she wanted to do was to go home

156

to England, and forget she had ever set eyes on Claude Girard!

"We have some news to tell you," Madame was saying with a smile. Tania looked quickly at Monique. Another wedding, maybe? She hoped so, because it would lessen the impact on this nice family when her own ended. But Monique and Denis hadn't yet set the date, she discovered.

"There has been a letter from Switzerland." Monique's voice had a raw tremor in it now. "From the clinic, Claude. The doctor there thinks there is some new treatment for Henri, which will take several weeks. Then, if that is successful, he can go ahead with an operation. The treatment has to work first, otherwise the operation is not possible. He explains it in some detail, but I cannot – I cannot dare to hope, I am afraid to hope— "

She handed the letter to Claude with shaking hands. Tania felt an infinite compassion for his sister. How terrible to watch a much-loved child condemned to lie in a wheelchair, and how well she understood Monique's fear for Henri. If the treatment failed, and his hopes were dashed, how much worse it would be for him.

"Have you told Henri?" Claude said, when he had skimmed through the letter. "How does he feel about treatment? The doctor says it will be uncomfortable at the very minimum."

"He can't wait." Monique gave a small smile. "He wants to climb a mountain, Claude. This treatment and operation will be my mountain. I dread it more than he does – but how can I refuse it? If all goes well, Henri will be as straight and tall as any other child in a few months' time. No-one has the right to deny him the chance."

Tania admired her courage, especially when she was

157

shown the doctor's letter, and realised that the treatment would be quite an ordeal for the boy. But it was vitally necessary, to allow the surgeons access to the wasted muscle and tissue in the child's back. It would mean days spent immobile, and she asked Monique when they had to give the doctor an answer.

"I have already given it," she replied. "This letter came three days ago, and there is a bed at the clinic for Henri in ten days' time. Denis and I have booked rooms at a nearby hotel for the weekend. I shall stay there for the whole time, so that I can see Henri every day, and Denis will come every weekend. If all goes well, the operation will take place before Christmas."

Her hands were clenched together, and it was obvious that there was only one Christmas present Monique wanted that year, and that was to see Henri well and strong again. Compared with that, other problems dwindled to so much trivia, Tania thought humbly.

"When it's time for the operation to take place, I shall go to Switzerland as well," Madame Girard declared. "Monique will be glad of some family support."

"*If* it takes place, Mother," Monique murmured, but Madame waved her aside with dogged determination.

"I refuse to doubt it. Henri will walk again, and climb his mountain, and I want to be there when the doctor tells him so," Madame said. There was a shine of tears in her eyes.

"Tania and I will be there too," Claude said. "At such a time a family needs to be together."

Monique's unspoken gratitude stopped Tania's turbulent thoughts that she may not even be part of the family by Christmas. It was no time to be letting such a thing creep into her mind. Nor to let herself feel sorrow washing

158

over her that this family was so very different from her own, sharing the good times and the bad, supporting each other with their strength and presence. How many times had she longed for her own parents, or her brother, to be there when she needed them? And how often had she struggled on alone? She said as much to Claude a long time later, when they went upstairs to bed, and she realised that all her belongings had been transferred to Claude's large room on the other side of the connecting door. Feeling slightly embarrassed at it all, she lay stiffly by his side, realising that with Henri's news, and the journey from Paris, he was in no mood to make love to her that night. She was glad. There were too many other things on her mind.

"I envy you your family, Claude," she said, feeling the familiar warmth of thigh touching thigh beneath the sheets.

"Why? Because they care about each other? There's nothing unusual in that." He sounded oddly belligerent, ready to argue, despite the late hour.

"Don't you believe it!" Tania muttered. She felt his breath on her cheek as he turned his face towards her in the soft darkness.

"Your parents cared about you. James cared. He told me often enough."

"They never stopped risking their necks for my sake, did they?" she whipped back, hurt, remembering.

"Did you ever go halfway to understanding why they did what they did?" Claude demanded. "Your parents were conservationists in the best sense of the word. They saved countless lives by their studies and reports, in the same way that James contributed to humanity by joining the mountain rescue team. You should be proud of them."

159

"In other words, I'm totally useless and inadequate, compared with them! It didn't matter that in caring for the wider world, they neglected those closest to home, did it?" She was too angry at his lack of understanding to be surprised at just how much he knew about her family.

"Just when are you going to stop using your childish rebellion as a prop?" Claude asked her calmly.

Tania froze beside him, her mind refusing to listen. She didn't understand what he meant, anyway. How could she be using her resentment at her family's way of life as a prop? Against what? Against whom?

"Think about it, Tania," he went on. "You're like a child with a comfort blanket. You refuse to go out and face the big wide world because it's easier to say it killed your parents and your brother. You won't take any chances, just because they did. If they had been recluses, would you have rebelled just as fast by being a total extrovert?"

"Of course I wouldn't. Don't be so ridiculous."

Claude shifted slightly away from her in the big double bed. She could feel him looking at her, although his face was only a shadowy blur in the night. Inside her chest, her heart was thumping painfully fast, as he forced her to examine her own motivation for living. She didn't want to do it. She preferred her prop . . . unwillingly the word trembled in her mind, but he hadn't done with her yet.

"Then perhaps you should ask yourself if they were rejecting you, or you were rejecting them, *chérie*." The endearment held no warmth.

"What! Of course I wasn't. How many times must I explain? I thought you understood. Oh, what does it matter, anyway? All of them are dead. Words can't bring them back." She bit her lips, feeling them tremble.

160

"I do understand. I understand that you were jealous of them."

"Jealous!" The word exploded from her lips. "Have you any other crazy ideas to label me with? I can't think why you married me, if I'm such a dead loss!"

"I didn't say that, Tania." Suddenly, he leaned across and kissed her mouth with a gentleness that brought a lump to her throat. "Go to sleep. We have work to do tomorrow."

He seemed able to switch off at will, she thought bitterly. It didn't matter that she lay, sleepless, no longer comforted by the sound of his breathing and the steady rise and fall of his chest. Nor later, when she had turned on her side, by the now familiar settling of her body into the curve of his, with his arms encircling her, his hands lightly holding her breasts as he slept.

What did he know of the torment she had gone through, during those years when she longed to turn to her mother with her growing-up problems, only to remember that she and her father were off in some God-forsaken hot country, examining the soil and insect life for posterity? Or how she had yearned for James's more matter-of-fact acceptance of the situation, and the maturity that came to him more easily than it did to Tania?

Slowly, painfully, it came to her at last that Claude could be right. She did use her resentment as a prop. She had been jealous of James's masculine ability to cope with a situation that she could not. All this time she had thought of her family's deaths as being a dire warning to herself. They were wrong to risk life and limb on their chosen roads, and she was right to be cautious, to want to be safe . . .

Now, at last, she saw that it was because in reality

she wished she could be like them, if only she had the nerve to take that leap into space from her safe shelf. It was why she had never been able to give David Lee the encouragement he had hoped for, because something basic within her told her this was wrong. There was more, much more – there was Claude. And Claude didn't really want her, except as a mother for his future children. She had made a hopeless mess of her life. For all that her parents and James had died, at least their lives had not been wasted. They had lived gloriously, and knew it was worth the risks. Tania finally knew it too.

If she thought her self-revelation was going to make some great significance in their lives, she was mistaken. Instead of feeling closer to Claude, his own attitude over the next weeks drove them farther apart. It was as if he was suddenly resentful of her being there, and apart from the work on the book, which was making steady progress, they behaved with studied politeness towards one another. It was all so wrong, Tania thought tragically. It was less harrowing when they ranted and raged at each other. At least then she was sure that he felt something towards her, if it was only anger. This way, he seemed coldly indifferent, except sometimes in the darkness of the night, when his arms would pull her close, and the mutual needs that wouldn't be denied became poignantly sweet. A man like Claude couldn't deny his own physical desires, when the woman in his arms shared his bed, and his name, and she was helpless to refuse him.

Sometimes, Tania suspected that he made love to her almost apologetically, as if unable to stop himself, yet sensing that all this, their marriage, her presence here, was only an interlude. That, when she chose, Tania would be gone from his life, for ever. The words were never spoken, but they hung between them like a great hovering cloud. His face was often drawn and unhappy, and Tania knew he was worried about the outcome of Henri's treatment. If the operation was impossible, it would be a bitter disappointment to all of them.

The time for Henri's departure was very near when the weather abruptly changed. One day, the trees were still fiery with autumn tints; the next, they were bare and chill, and the first snows of winter came shivering through the valley. Already the mountains were crowned with white, and the winter climbing season would begin. There had been consultations in Claude's study, with his bright young assistant, Marc, and the other members of the rescue team, who operated at various places throughout the area, connected by phone and ready at a moment's notice to converge on the various base camps where a rescue was needed. Tania prayed the day wouldn't come just yet.

"Thank goodness the snow isn't settling yet," Monique observed as she and Henri prepared to leave in the car when the time came. The boy was pale, but excited too, unheeding of anything but the fact that soon he too might climb a mountain like his adored uncle. Tania's throat was thick, hearing his non-stop chatter. No risks were too great, if the end justified the means. If only she and Claude were less distant towards each other, she would tell him she knew it now. But they didn't share that kind of closeness lately.

"You'll be fine with Alphonse driving," Madame assured Monique. "We shall be thinking of you all the time, my dear ones."

"You'll all come to the clinic to see me walk when I've had the operation, won't you?" Henri said eagerly.

163

Tania's throat tightened at his confident little face. She prayed that all would go well. She hugged Monique and Denis as they prepared to leave. Alphonse would drive the three of them to Bordeaux, and they would fly to Geneva. The clinic bordered Lake Geneva, and Monique promised to phone home each night to report Henri's progress.

At the last moment, Henri swivelled in his wheelchair to come close to Tania. He reached up to her, his arms clinging round her neck for a kiss, as he whispered in her ear in a fair English accent.

"When I come home, will you teach me more about England, Tania? When I can walk, Claude says he will take me there."

"We'll both take you," she heard herself say unsteadily. "It's a promise, darling."

She didn't think Claude had heard. She didn't really know why she had said it. She hadn't needed to. The child would have been satisfied with a lesser response. She only knew that at that moment she had wanted to give him all the support she could, and the continuity of knowing that when he returned, well and strong, everything would be the same. It was what she had always wanted for herself. If she hadn't ever achieved it, at least she could give the promise to the child. It was the most precious gift that she could make.

Much later, when sleep was difficult, wondering about Henri, despite the fact that Monique had phoned to say they had arrived safely at the clinic and Henri had the company of several other small boys, Tania moved restlessly in the bed beside Claude. She thought he was asleep, but evidently he too was wakeful, because his voice sounded strong and unrelaxed when it came to her in the darkness.

"You shouldn't make promises you can't keep, *chérie*. It's better not to make them at all."

The words trembled on her tongue that of course she meant to keep her promise to Henri. Did he think so little of her? Then she felt instinctively that his words had a deeper meaning. Their own promises to love and cherish, said such a little while ago, were as insubstantial as the first snows of winter.

Without words, Tania knew that Claude was well aware that she would leave him. She could interpret foreign languages with fluent ease, but she was unable to fathom out any inflexion in her own husband's voice at that moment. He made no attempt to help her. He turned his back on her and muttered a curt goodnight. The slow curling tears ran silently around her cheeks, more bitter than gall.

Chapter 10

The next few weeks were difficult ones for Tania. Each member of the Girard family seemed to be enclosed in a private world of anxiety. The first treatment sessions on Henri weren't too encouraging, and had to be started all over again. Monique's phone calls to her mother and to Claude were sometimes tearful, and Tania felt very much the outsider. She longed to give Claude some comfort, but he didn't ask it of her, and he seemed too wrapped up in his own affairs lately to care what she did.

He was often away from the château, on meetings with his fellow mountain rescue team organisers. Winter was coming in fast, and the fascination for the mountains was insidiously creeping into Claude's dinner conversation. Tania recognised it only too well. She had heard that same enthusiasm in her brother's voice, so many times. She had never thought she would understand it. But strangely, little by little, as she and Claude had worked in his study together for the first draft of his book, she realised she had come to terms with a man's need to conquer an environment outside his own little space of home and family. He was still the hunter.

Four weeks after Monique and Henri had gone to the Swiss clinic, the phone rang while Tania was alone. She

166

picked it up, to hear Monique's voice, laughing and crying at the same time.

"The doctor has given us the go-ahead for the operation, Tania," she gabbled so quickly, Tania could hardly understand her rapid French, but the gist of it was loud and clear.

"Oh, how wonderful. When?" She hardly got the chance to ask.

"Not for another two weeks, so I shall be staying on here, of course. It makes such a difference to Henri to have me near – and Denis too, at the weekends. Denis has been so wonderful – a tower of strength – everything a father could be to Henri."

Tania heard Monique's voice soften, hesitate, and then rush on.

"I wasn't going to say anything yet, Tania, but I think of you as a sister, and I must tell you. When all this is over, and Henri is walking tall and strong, Denis and I will be married. It will take some time for Henri to regain the use of wasted muscles, and he will have to learn to walk again. But it will happen, Tania, I know it will. And probably in the spring, Denis and I will be married. I would like it very much if you will be my attendant. Please say that you will."

How could she possibly say that by the spring she intended being far away from here? Running away from reality, as she had always done . . . the imaginary words were all in her head, in Claude's angry voice. Tania brushed them away, telling Monique how happy she would be to act as bridal attendant. There would be time enough later for Monique to find someone else. Now was not the time to distress her when she was so keyed-up over Henri, both elated and apprehensive.

167

She relayed the news to Madame Girard and Claude over dinner that evening. By now, the château fireplaces glowed with great burning logs every evening to warm the chilled air, and the tangy scent brought a breath of Christmas to Tania's nostrils, though it was still some time away yet. When it came, where would she be? Still here, caught up in an impossible situation, loving a man who seemed to have turned against her completely in everything but business matters? Back in England, enmeshed in the cloying Lee household? No, that was one place she wouldn't be, Tania thought decisively. It was about the only thing she was certain of these days.

"I shall go to Lucerne when the operation is due," Madame declared at once. "A family should be together at such times, and Monique will need our support."

"Of course, Mother," Claude agreed. "Tania and I will accompany you. Henri has become so fond of her, I know it will please him."

She didn't answer, murmuring a brief acknowledgement. He hadn't asked her whether or not she wanted to go. She was his wife, and it was expected of her. His wife . . . she looked across the dazzling white tablecloth, the heavy Girard silver gleaming in the glow of firelight and the tall candelabra, seeing opposite her the face of the man she loved more wildly, more completely, than she had ever dreamed it possible to love a man. The soft lighting threw the planes and contours of his face into rugged shadows. As rugged as the mountains he loved. Tania felt a sudden stinging jealousy for the mountains, as pointless as it was sharp and real. Claude showed them all the care and consideration and respect that he would give to a woman. Right now, the mountains had his love too. At least, Tania had none of it . . .

He looked up from his meal, and over the rim of his wine glass, their eyes met. Tania's prickled a little, wishing she could read of his love in the dark depths. Why had he married her? Why? He had desired her, wanted her with a passion that had dazzled her senses, but it wasn't love, it wasn't the same as love, that tenderest, most beautiful of emotions. Love lasted for ever, while desire could wane and die. She hid a small sob, because it was painfully obvious now that that was just what had happened. Claude's desire had been sated, and he had been willing to pay the price of marrying her to get what he wanted, since it was rejected in any other way. And now he was resenting the fact. He was cold towards her, rarely making love to her, and it was Tania who yearned for his touch, his warmth, his love. He had allowed her to blossom into womanhood, to be more aware of herself and of life, and he had just as coolly left her wanting. It was cruel and arrogant, but her pride wouldn't let her make any approaches towards him. Let him think she was happy enough with their new arrangement. Let him think she didn't care for him, as she had made it plain enough in the beginning. She lowered her amber eyes from his steady gaze.

The day of Henri's operation drew near. It would be a delicate operation, and there was no denying the air of anxiety in the family. Monique welcomed the fact that the others would be there to support her in the hours of awaiting the result. Even now, it could fail, and Henri would be doomed to the wheelchair once more, unless the surgeon decided he could try again. But she wouldn't think of that, Monique had said bravely on the phone. She wouldn't think of failure, only of seeing Henri walk again. As she had once said, this was her mountain. Tania admired her tremendously. She had all Claude's strength of character in her slender body, and God willing, Henri had it too, to help him through his ordeal. He was so little, so vulnerable . . .

Madame and Claude and Tania were to leave for Lucerne in two days' time. The roads were slippery with snow now, and Alphonse had fitted snow-chains to the wheels of the limousine. He would take them all to Bordeaux airport. They intended to stay for a week or less, just to see the operation through, and ensure that he was on the road to recovery. Claude didn't want to be away any longer. Already the winter sports enthusiasts were invading the slopes of the Pyrenees, and there had been isolated calls for help, minor ones so far, but the threat of danger was ever present as jagged slopes that had once provided good footholds turned into precipitous sheets of glacial ice. More often than not, Claude had spent his time at the well-equipped base camp at the foot of the favoured climbing ranges, to be within reach of a mayday call with his team.

Reputable climbing teams checked in with the rescue headquarters before they set out, giving detailed charts and routes, and estimated times and distances to be covered, so that any irregularities could be charted and suspected at once. Unfortunately, not all climbers bothered with such sensible requirements, preferring to go it alone in a false sense of pioneering and adventure.

The morning of the departure to Lucerne arrived, and so did the high-pitched buzzing of the alarm bell in Claude's operations room. Tania felt her heart turn over as she heard it, and followed Claude into the now familiar room, to hear him speak rapidly into the phone, his fingers tracing over the large-scale map of the Pyrenees mountain range, covering the whole of one wall.

From his angry exclamations and the stabbing fingers on the map, Tania guessed there was something badly wrong. She heard him speaking Marc's name, telling him quickly that he would be there as fast as he could, and not to worry about the other matter, because Claude would take care of it.

A sixth sense seemed to tie Tania's stomach up in knots at that moment. She couldn't have explained the reason for it. It was a bit like the seconds just prior to a storm, when everything seemed to be waiting, hushed, yet crackling with undercurrents of the tension to come. Claude looked at her calmly.

How could he be so calm, she thought fleetingly, when all her instincts told her this was the big one, the rescue call she had been inwardly dreading all these months? She had hardly registered the fact until now, when the moment was here, shivering in the air between them. For some crazy reason she suddenly remembered young Henri's face lighting up, telling her of some of Claude's rescues, his childish pride, the confines of the wheelchair doing nothing to diminish the male need to dominate the very elements, to cheat the greedy mountains of death. James hadn't cheated them, she thought, with bitter pain. The mountains had won, and now Claude, Claude . . . A wave of emotion caught her throat. Not again, not again. She stepped forward, her hand reaching out to touch his arm, the words trembling on her lips to beg him not to go, not to do this. She was ashamed of her cowardly feelings, and for daring to voice them to Claude, but this was her love, her very life . . . Before she could say anything, Claude spoke, his voice hard, unemotional now, seeing only the job that had to be done.

"No doubt you heard some of that, Tania. I'm needed at once."

"Is there no-one else?" she said tremblingly. "Must it be you?" She bit her lip at his look.

"Your consideration does you credit, *chérie*, but it's a little late to pretend a wifely concern. Alphonse must take Mother to the airport alone."

The significance of the remark hadn't yet reached her mind.

"But Henri, the operation— " She was still clutching at straws to make him stay with her.

"Henri is in the best of hands at the clinic. The team of three Dutch climbers is relaying messages that one of them has fallen down a deep fissure and the others can't reach him. There's danger of an avalanche." He spoke in clipped, precise tones, all the while collecting data from his files, relevant information as to exact rock formations, snowfalls, current wind speeds and directions. All the things Tania had begun to learn about since being here. She knew the dangers more acutely now. "Would you have me leave them to their fate when I have intimate knowledge of their position and hopefully can help them? Is that what you'd have wanted for James, while would-be rescuers pursued personal desires?"

That was cruel. The salt tears stung her eyes, when suddenly she felt the grip of Claude's strong hands on her arms, his eyes seeming to bore into hers, willing her to understand, as if it was necessary to him that she should.

"Can't you see that I must do this, for James, for me, for every damn-fool man who ever wanted to climb a mountain, Tania? Even for Henri . . . I could go to the clinic, and stand by with the rest of you while the operation takes place, but it's not my way to stand by when I can be useful to someone. I'm needed in the mountains. *Needed* – do you understand what that means?"

"Yes. I do. Oh Claude, I do." The blood seemed to rush through her veins, hot and turbulent. To be needed was to be loved. She needed too, but she could no longer fight the needs she felt in him. She had to let him go. She would accompany his mother to Lucerne and share the watchful hours.

"I need you with me." His next words stunned her, and she felt as if her face paled, then flooded with colour. He gave a twisted smile. "Don't worry, I'm not asking you to put on climbing boots in the physical sense. But these crazy Dutchmen only know a smattering of French, and are having great difficulty making themselves understood. It will be almost impossible to give precise instructions to them unless they can follow them exactly."

Tania's mouth was so dry she could hardly move her lips. "What – what do you expect me to do? I – I can't, Claude, don't ask this of me."

"There's no-one else. You have to come. You'll be quite safe. You'll stay at base camp with the controller, who will instruct you in the three-way radio system. Everything you hear me say to the climbers must be translated into Dutch, and their own replies passed back to me. You're an expert linguist, Tania. It will save hours of valuable time if you come with me now. It may very well save lives."

Her heart thudded violently. It was all her worst nightmares rolled into one, to be personally involved with the mountains, and to feel so sickeningly that she had no choice, no choice at all. She owed it to James's memory. Claude released her, and Tania felt strangely as if she stood alone for the first time in her life, yet it didn't hurt. She was the symbol of Henri's future, standing without props, moving forward, dictating the terms of her life.

"What are we waiting for?" she said huskily.

The next thirty-six hours were the most traumatic of Tania's life. She and Claude drove to the mountain rescue base camp as quickly as the slippery roads would allow. Overhead the sky was a grey canopy; before them reared the towering, snow-clad mountains, majestic and terrifying. At their foot, Tania felt dwarfed, dehumanised, cold to her bones. Marc awaited them with three others, equipped with all the mountaineering gear, the helmets and snow-goggles, climbing irons and ropes, the medical equipment and stretchers, brandy and food and tents. The thought of carrying all that across a road was enough to make ordinary men quake a little, let alone to the places Tania found unimaginable. For the first time, she gave them all her unstinted admiration.

There was little time for anything else. She was quickly initiated into the three-way radio system by a fresh-faced young Frenchman called Eduard. They were the anchormen, Claude told her jocularly. For a moment he pulled her close to him, as the others tactfully turned their backs.

"We make it a practice never to say goodbye," he said roughly. "So it's *au revoir, chérie*, until we meet again."

He held her tight. Through the thick layers of clothing he wore, she imagined she could feel the strong beat of his heart next to hers. His hands pushed carelessly through the tumble of her hair. His touch made her scalp tingle. She clung to him wordlessly, wanting to say so much . . . so much . . . and capable of saying nothing at all. He swore softly, and for a brief moment his cheek rested against hers, the roughness of it instantly familiar and dear to her, making her throat thicken. Was all this just for effect, because the others would expect him to kiss his wife goodbye? The thought wouldn't leave her, although it made her want to weep.

"I love you," Claude said in a swift whisper against her cheek, and seconds later he was rejoining the others, leaving her with Eduard, cheerfully asking her if she would like some coffee, while Tania replied mechanically, hearing nothing, seeing nothing, wondering if she had really heard those whispered words, or if her own longing had conjured them up out of her own imagination. Her heart had leapt, only to resume beating crazily fast. She *had* heard them, felt them, against her skin . . .

Why had Claude said he loved her? Was it because it was what he knew she wanted to hear, handed to her like a little talisman as he went on his dangerous mission? There had been no need. He was the one in danger, not Tania. And yet, didn't her heart go with him, every step of the way? Didn't he know it? But of course he didn't, because she had made it plain to him that she hated him and what he did. She resented the fact that she had married him because of a moment's weakness at seeing him in the throes of a nightmare. She was frightened of what was happening, up there, in the unknown, in the silent world of the mountains that had killed her brother. Most of all, she was frightened for Claude.

She knew exactly what he had meant now, when he said Henri was in good hands, and Claude was most needed

175

here. James, too, was beyond anyone's help, anyone's love, and it was futile to look backwards, when all the future beckoned. If they *had* a future after today. Tania repulsed all negative thoughts, took the scalding coffee from Eduard, and asked what she had to do.

Throughout the whole process of the rescue, Tania was emotionally and professionally involved, part of Claude's world, and in being a part of it, she began to understand it. From the first moment she made radio contact with the three Dutchmen in the mountains, and heard their astonishment and then their varied reactions at hearing a woman's voice speaking to them in their own language, Tania was held in an urgent need to help in any way she could. There were even moments when the Dutchmen made joking passes at her over the air, and to keep up their spirits, she responded, only to have Claude's crackling voice intervening with mild comments to keep her mind on the job.

It was nerve-racking, tensely scaring, exhilarating and emotional. To speak to Claude, knowing that at any moment they may lose contact, and knowing that the reason could be a mere loss of radio signal, or a fatal one, was more heart-palpitating than anything Tania had ever known before. But the strange thing about it was her own reaction to her position here. Gradually as time passed, she began to realise she wouldn't want to be anywhere else. If she had been left at the château while all this drama was happening, she would be frustrated and helpless. Here, she was needed, as she had never been needed before. If she never shared another thing with Claude, she was grateful for having been allowed to share this.

He would be triumphant if she ever dared to tell

him so! She and James were more alike than she had realised. And her parents too . . . she knew now how their hunger to seek knowledge from the world they had chosen from themselves could never be swamped by domesticity, however much they loved their children. These hours fraught with danger had taught her so much more than a lifetime's academic learning.

"We've got them!" Claude's jubilant voice suddenly came over the radio. "They're all right. A bit bruised and battered, but no worse. We're coming in – hold on, one of them has something to say." Claude evidently allowed one of the rescued men to speak.

He spoke in Dutch, as Tania had heard the voice all that gruelling day and part of the night. She knew his voice so well now, and suddenly she realised the message was for her alone.

"Thank you, lovely lady," the man said, his voice rough with emotion. "You were our inspiration. Will you marry me?"

Tania laughed, and it seemed as if her jaw ached with the strangeness of the sound. It had been tensed for hours.

"Tell him no," Claude put in, suddenly aggressive. "Tell him you're spoken for."

She did so, feeling a quiver run through her. Was she? Now that the worst was over and the descent could begin, there was time to remember other things. Like the fact that Claude had said "I love you", and held her close, and stirred up all the longings she had kept hidden recently. There was time, too, to remember Henri, and to wonder how the operation had gone. She left Eduard in charge of the radio now, and put through a phone call to the clinic. Minutes later, she was feeling another flood of thankfulness as she learned that the operation had been a complete success.

As soon as she could, she relayed the news to Claude. He said little, but she recognised the gladness in his voice. Tania hesitated, then she added softly, "Some day he'll be able to climb his mountain, Claude."

He was too busy to reply. There was still a hazardous return journey, and she and Eduard seemed to have drunk an endless amount of coffee. She was suddenly ravenous, and Eduard produced some tins of soup and a loaf of bread, and Tania heated it on the small gas stove. It tasted like nectar.

At last the climbers and the rescuers came back to the base camp, and Tania was hugged by the three brawny Dutchman, not too exhausted to appreciate the sight of a pretty woman, and to make it clear how much they envied Claude Girard his lady. She blushed, hearing them, glad that the others weren't fully aware of all that they said. They would sleep here now, and leave in the morning. Claude looked at Tania.

"Can we go home?" she said tremulously. He nodded, and she still couldn't be sure whether their relationship had changed or not. She sat beside him in his car as he sped silently through the snow-covered countryside in the pale unearthly light of dawn. It was hours since they had slept, and her whole body felt stiff and aching, her eyes gritty. Claude must feel so much more exhausted than she did. They spoke little on the journey, and now she wondered if he regretted his impulsive words. He had said he loved her. If it was all a lie, she just couldn't bear to know it. Not yet. She was still too emotionally fragile, still somewhere high on the mountain . . .

"We will talk later," Claude said, when they reached the

château. "We have things to discuss. They cannot remain unsaid any longer, Tania. But we are both desperate for sleep, and I think that is our first priority."

Tania nodded. What things did they have to discuss, she thought uneasily? He looked so serious, so fatigued. She longed to smooth away the deep-etched lines of tension from his face, but she was afraid to be so intimate with him. He looked oddly detached, even deflated. Maybe it was the aftermath of the rescue, where all his strength had been demanded of him, but there was a gnawing feeling inside her that if he wanted to discuss releasing her from their marriage, she just couldn't bear it.

She couldn't blame him if it was what he thought she wanted. She had intimated as much enough times. What a blind fool she had been. But she still had to know a few things for herself, and she needed to be in full control of her faculties before then. Sleep must come first.

Someone had lit a fire in their bedroom and kept it going until their return, and the room was warm and welcoming. Claude took a quick shower, and while Tania did the same to ease her taut muscles, he phoned down to the staff to thank them for the fire in the room, saying that he would ring down when they needed anything more. The words drifted in and out of Tania's senses as she fell into bed, and was asleep almost immediately. She could think of nothing else but the bliss of being warm and relaxed . . .

It was brilliant daylight when she awoke, a crystal-clear day made sparkling by thin rays of December sunlight on the frozen snow. In the fireplace the fire still burned, and Tania realised that Claude must have put more logs on it, at some time. She turned her head fractionally, stretching her limbs carefully, and finding that she was still supple after all, after the rigours of the time spent huddled over the radio in the base camp.

Her heart jolted as her eyes encountered Claude's. Next to her on the pillow, he was fully awake, but unmoving, and she had the odd feeling that he had been watching her sleep. The trite "good morning" stuck in her throat, and instead she lay very still, breathless, waiting . . . yet not still at all, for every nerve-end inside her was tingling and alive, as if her whole body was aware that these moments were very important ones. Her body recognised it as much as her mind.

"I want to thank you, Tania," he said quietly. "It was cruel of me to drag you along with me, but there was nothing else I could do. I know what an ordeal it must have been for you."

He had thanked her once before, when he had made love to her. She had thought it was an insult, instead of a sharing of mind and spirit. This time she felt it was her failure, that he should think it necessary. Her amber eyes blurred to a liquid fire.

"It's you that I should thank, Claude," she whispered painfully. "For making me see that I've been a child all this time, hiding behind my own inadequacy. I was afraid to reach out and discover just what I was capable of being. I know now."

She ached now with a different kind of hunger. To feel his arms around her, to know his caresses and the sweet warm familiarity of his love-making. She had to know if he really loved her . . .

"Claude," her mouth trembled as she spoke his name, "you said something before you left me at base camp. Did you mean it?"

For a moment she saw the defensive look come into his

eyes, and didn't understand it. "I'm sorry if it bothered you," he said raggedly. "Put it down to a feeling of premonition, that I had better say it once, just in case I never got the chance to say it again."

She put her soft fingers against his mouth. She couldn't bear him to tease her now, even though she didn't need telling that there was no laughter in him at that moment. He was as tense as she was, and that gave her hope.

"But did you mean it?" she whispered. "Did you? Don't I have the right to know? I am your wife!"

She drew in her breath as the look in his eyes darkened at her words. So suddenly she hardly knew how it had happened, he had pulled her towards him in one fluid movement, so that she lay above him as he stared up into her face, his dark eyes searching hers, as her hair cascaded about her shoulders and his. She heard and felt the sudden pounding of his heartbeats beneath her own. And even before he spoke, Tania was aware of a sudden surge of exultation, as if all the ice around her heart was melting . . .

"Yes, I meant it! When do I say anything I don't mean? I love you, and I've loved you for a very long time, ever since James used to tell me about his beautiful sister. I've seen your face in my dreams a thousand times, knowing it so well from the photos James showed me. I didn't recognise the feelings as love, not until I met you in London, and you let me know only too well what you thought of me and how you despised me. I couldn't bear to know you thought so ill of me, but even then I had no real intention of taking things this far, I swear it. Forcing you into a marriage you didn't want must be one of the worst tricks a man can play on a woman."

"I didn't have to accept! I still had a mind of my own. I could have said no – if I had wanted to."

While he had been talking, his eyes had become haunted again, the way they had been during the nightmare, his movements suddenly restless, tortured. At her words, his eyes focused on her face again, on the soft tremulous mouth and the love that shone out of her eyes as if a thousand fires were lit behind them. His voice was velvety now, sending wild shivers of excitement through her veins. She was conscious of the warmth of his flesh touching hers, wanting hers, and love and desire were intermingled on his face in the most beautiful look of all.

"Why didn't you say no?" Claude asked her. She could feel the small movements of his hands along her spine, possessing her as surely as spring followed winter. She felt so loved she wanted to cry, except that she didn't want to cry, she wanted . . . she wanted . . .

"Because I love you." She spoke the words to him for the first time, tasting them, loving the sound of them, the feel of them on her lips. "I love you, Claude, so much, so very much."

She couldn't say more, because by then his mouth was crushing hers, and she felt as if she was spinning slowly in space as he reversed their positions in slow motion, never loosening his hold on her, as if he would never let her out of his arms again.

The sense of wonder pervaded every part of her, awakening her as from a long deep sleep, for now at last she knew the joy of love, and the ecstacy of belonging to one man, one love, now and for always.

R